The Journey North

THE 15TH ALABAMA FIGHTS
THE 20TH MAINE AT GETTYSBURG

"I expect to maintain this contest until successful, or till I die, or am conquered, or my term expires, or Congress or the country forsake me."

PRESIDENT ABRAHAM LINCOLN

"Ours is not a revolution. We are a free and independent people, in States that had the right to make a better government when they saw fit."

PRESIDENT JEFFERSON DAVIS, C.S.A.

"No man has greater love than he who lays down his life for a friend."

JOHN 15:13

Sam,
Enjoy your read!
Peter [signature]

The Journey North

THE 15TH ALABAMA FIGHTS
THE 20TH MAINE AT GETTYSBURG

Written by

PETER WARREN

ROY MCKINNEY AND EDWARD ODOM

WestBow
PRESS
A DIVISION OF THOMAS NELSON

WestBow Press books may be ordered through booksellers or by contacting:

WestBow Press
A Division of Thomas Nelson
1663 Liberty Drive
Bloomington, IN 47403
www.westbowpress.com
1-(866) 928-1240

This fictional piece of work, while including many accurate historical facts, also includes fictional characters, conversations, writings (in the form of letters), and dialogues which take place between characters in the book. They are not intended to be real or historically accurate. They are a product of the authors' imaginations and are intended solely to enhance the book's story line. Some scenes, events, and locations, within the book have also been created for the same reason.

ISBN: 978-1-4497-8591-8 (e)
ISBN: 978-1-4497-8592-5 (sc)
ISBN: 978-1-4497-8593-2 (hc)

Library of Congress Control Number: 2013903101

Printed in the United States of America

WestBow Press rev. date: 04/05/2013

Peter Warren is also the author of *Confederate Gold and Silver.*
readpfw@yahoo.com
http://www.readpete.com
See the author's Facebook page for additional information.
Twitter: @peterfwarren

Roy McKinney
roy.mckinney@me.com
See the author's Facebook page for additional information
Twitter: @rmckinn

Edward Odom
edwardlodom@gmail.com
See the author's Facebook page for additional information

Painting by Don Troiani, www.historicalimagebank.com

Individuals and/or organizations that are interested in having
any of the authors speak at one of your events or functions
may contact them directly or through WestBow Press.

For information about this book, please visit
us at www.thejourneynorth.net

TABLE OF CONTENTS

DEDICATION PAGE

To the two ladies in my life, Debra Warren and Rita Warren.
Thank you both for the support you have given to me.

In memory of William B. Skelton, Jr.,
Capt., U.S. Army, 1920 – 2011, who touched many lives.

To my late wife, Hazel Hamilton Odom,
who was by my side for 35 years.

ACKNOWLEDGEMENTS

During the course of our long friendship, we have had many occasions to sit and talk about our respective interests in the American Civil War. On many occasions, we also have been fortunate enough to have done so with several of our mutual friends. From these talks, we each have learned a great deal more about the war, and have learned a great deal more about each other as well.

Like the principle characters in our book, William Barton and Louis Hiram Pierce, we each share many mutual interests together despite coming from three somewhat different backgrounds. During our friendship, we have always lived in different sections of the country, each a significant distance away from each other. Despite that inconvenience, we have managed to remain friends by staying in contact with each other on a regular basis. Often it has happened due to our interest in the Civil War. Each of us has our opinions about the war, our own favorite battles, and our own favorite personalities.

The one thing we each have had in common since the time we first started sharing our interests in the war with each other is that we have always had a deep respect for the soldiers who participated in the war. While time has not diminished the names of people like Abraham Lincoln or Robert E. Lee, or the names of the other famous generals from the war, and while recent movies, such as *Gettysburg*, and *Lincoln*, have made us more aware of the contributions of others in the war, people like Union Generals Joshua Lawrence Chamberlain and Ulysses S. Grant, or Confederate General James Longstreet, time has often forgotten the contributions of the common soldier who served both causes so admirably, and often with undying devotion. We have not done that. While this book is centered on two fictional characters, their roles are quite similar to those many soldiers that served their respective sides during the war.

Several of the fictional characters in this book are named after mutual friends of ours. These friends, people like Jeffrey Brandau, Timothy Baughman, and Kent Wilson, are Civil War buffs like us. They all have been great friends of ours for years. To them, we extend our sincere appreciation for allowing us to make them a part of the story we have told.

To our wives, Debbie, and Mindy, and to the memory of Hazel Odom, we express our sincere thanks for your support and love over the past many years. We could not have written this book without you. And, to our mothers, Rita Warren, and Rosaleen McKinney, we sincerely appreciate your continued support and love.

The authors wish to extend their appreciation to Don Troiani, and to Robin Feret, at Historical Art Prints, for making it possible to use Mr. Troiani's painting, *Lions of the Roundtop*, as the front cover for our book.

FOREWORD

"The enemy has made a stand at Chancellor's which is about two miles from Chancellorsville. I hope as soon as possible to attack."

GENERAL THOMAS 'STONEWALL' JACKSON, MAY 2, 1863, ONLY HOURS BEFORE BEING MORTALLY WOUNDED BY HIS OWN TROOPS.

The passage of time has done little to stem the praises, as well as the criticism, of the men who fought so hard for their causes at Gettysburg. It is believed that thousands of books, articles, and essays, have been written just about that one three-day battle alone. Each writer has had his or her own thoughts and beliefs on what went right and what went wrong during that epic battle.

Gettysburg was only one of far too many battles that were fought during the American Civil War. While it occurred one hundred and fifty years ago this year, it remains as one of the focal points of the war. It remains as the largest, and bloodiest, battle ever fought on our nation's soil. While the fighting that took place on Days Two and Three remain among the most talked about, and certainly rank among the most documented battles that occurred there, Little Round Top did not have the biggest influence on the outcome of the three-day fight. To most historians, and to most Civil War buffs, Pickett's Charge remains as the most deciding factor of the events that unfolded in that small town in 1863.

Despite being poorly trained, and poorly equipped in all of the necessities of war as compared to the larger and stronger Union army, the Confederate army had performed admirably before coming to Gettysburg. Stunning victories over the Union army at Fredericksburg, and at Chancellorsville, had bolstered the confidence they had in their ability to persevere in this brutal war. As the war pitted the two large armies against each other, to a lesser degree, it was also one that often pitted family and friends against each other as well.

Turning his army to the north in the summer of 1863, both to threaten Washington, D.C., and other northern cities, and to obtain much needed supplies from the rich farmlands of Pennsylvania, General Robert E. Lee soon arrived in Gettysburg. It would prove to be a move that he would soon regret.

While the defeat of the Army of Northern Virginia has caused generations of scholars, historians, and Civil War buffs, to question the tactical decisions Lee made at Gettysburg, no one can ever challenge the bravery and courage of the vast number of soldiers who fought there. The unchallenged devotion to their leaders, and to the causes they believed in, resulted in acts of bravery that became the norm for so many soldiers who fought in that three-day battle.

This story focuses on two fictional characters, one from each of the two participants, who, by a strange twist of events, accidently meet at the scene of one of Gettysburg's most vicious fights. While the description of the events in this book are somewhat fictional at times, they also represent what actually transpired between the Union army's 20th Maine, and the Confederacy's 15th Alabama, during the bloody fight for Little Round Top.

The Confederacy's frontal assault upon Little Round Top remains as one of the most debated points regarding Lee's tactics during this historic battle. The assault over such difficult terrain resulted in the senseless slaughter of so many of General James Longstreet's soldiers. Barely twenty-four hours later, on Day Three, the Confederacy would again use another frontal assault against the Union line along Cemetery Ridge. That assault, most commonly known as Pickett's Charge, would also result in the slaughter of many Confederate soldiers.

The fight for Little Round Top has also resulted in the names of Major General Gouverneur Warren, General Joshua Chamberlain, Colonel Strong Vincent, Colonel William Oates, General James Longstreet, and the 20th Maine, as well as the 15th Alabama, to be remembered by the generations that followed theirs.

While the principle characters in this story are fictional, other characters, like those so previously mentioned, are real. Many participated, in some manner, in the fight for Little Round Top. Fictional or not, these soldiers, regardless of their rank or affiliation, personify the intense dedication that the actual combatants gave to the state's they fought for, and to those soldiers they fought alongside of. History has documented, as this story also has, that soldiers often put aside their adversarial roles to help others in great need. Such occasions help to define what the American spirit truly is all about.

Enjoy your reading!

Spring, 1861

I

CONJECTURE AND SPECULATION.

"Four score and seven years ago our fathers brought forth on this continent,
a new nation, conceived in Liberty, and dedicated to the proposition that
all men are created equal. Now we are engaged in a great civil war, testing
whether that nation, or any nation so conceived and so dedicated, can long
endure. We are met on a great battle-field of that war. We have come to
dedicate a portion of that field, as a final resting place for those who here
gave their lives that that nation might live. It is altogether fitting and proper
that we should do this. But, in a larger sense, we can not dedicate -- we can
not consecrate -- we can not hallow -- this ground. The brave men, living
and dead, who struggled here, have consecrated it, far above our poor power
to add or detract. The world will little note, nor long remember what we
say here, but it can never forget what they did here. It is for us the living,
rather, to be dedicated here to the unfinished work which they who fought
here have thus far so nobly advanced. It is rather for us to be here dedicated
to the great task remaining before us -- that from these honored dead we take
increased devotion to that cause for which they gave the last full measure of
devotion -- that we here highly resolve that these dead shall not have died
in vain -- that this nation, under God, shall have a new birth of freedom
-- and that government of the people, by the people, for the people, shall not
perish from the earth."

PRESIDENT ABRAHAM LINCOLN'S GETTYSBURG ADDRESS –
NOVEMBER 19, 1863

As the days dwindled in their numbers on the calendar of 1860, the talk of war between the nation's states grew stronger and stronger. What started as talk and idle threats soon led to a growing speculation that such a war was a strong likelihood. It became even more likely that war

1

would occur after the South, on two different dates, took drastic steps to secede from the Union. In December, South Carolina would adopt their ordinance of secession, and on February 18, 1861, in Montgomery, Alabama, the South inaugurated their first president. Many now felt that such speculation would soon become a strong probability by the spring of 1861.

No matter where you lived in that time of our nation's history, whether it was in the more industrialized northern states, such as New York, or those in New England, or on a farm in the agrarian sections of the rural South, talk of a looming war was news that reached you. Newspapers, telegraph operators, periodicals, and even word of mouth, told you about the coming war. Word of the pending war found you even if you were travelling westward in the expansion of our young new nation.

Like all types of fights, big or small, when talk of the fast approaching war reached the citizens of our country, it was then that they often made their decisions on which side to support. On most occasions, men generally chose to serve with those regiments that others from their hometowns, their cities, or their counties, had chosen to join. Most often it was with those regiments that their respective states had formed and called into service. In many cases it was the same regiment that their brothers, uncles, friends, and cousins had also chosen to serve with. It was not only men fighting for the causes they believed in, or for the causes they were told to believe in, but rather it was often about fighting to protect their family members, their friends, and their way of life. For some men, they knew little about the actual causes of the war. Many had simply joined out of loyalty to their respective states.

As war became a reality in the spring of 1861, men from all walks of life, from Maine to Alabama, would find it difficult not to fight when they were asked to do so. Failing to answer the Call to Arms, like failing to support the regiment that other members from your hometown had joined, was akin to faking an injury before a big battle. Not doing your part was something that would soon filter back to your hometown. It would be something that would tarnish your family name for years. During the war that soon would envelop the nation, men who were pushed to the end of their wits by the sights and sounds of bloody engagements would often rather perish in battle than to disgrace their family or community. It was a sense of duty, or perhaps it was a sense of responsibility, that existed during this period of time. It would not be rivaled until the nation called our men and women into service for World War II.

As the country went to war in April of 1861, cities, towns, and the many states across our great nation, just as the federal and Confederate governments had done, put out their own calls for thousands of volunteers to come help fight against their fellow countrymen. These calls went out to every community across the nation. Like those in other communities across the nation, men in Portland, Maine, and men from counties across Alabama, ones like Russell County, and Henry County, would soon answer the Call to Arms. Men from both of these states, some drafted, but mostly those who had volunteered just like so many others from across the nation, would not live to see July 4, 1863.

Two of these men, one from Maine, and one from Alabama, would live to see the nation's eighty-seventh birthday. They would both see it and experience it, but only by the grace of God. Those last few days leading up to that birthday would be ones they, and thousands of other soldiers just like them, would never forget. These were men who, in July of 1863, survived three days of brutal fighting. They would never forget what they had lived through. For most of those men, the memories of what they had experienced during those brutal days of fighting would be vividly remembered for years and years to come.

Like those brave soldiers who fought in the three-day battle leading up to July 4, 1863, the nation would also never forget what transpired on those bloody days of the war. Far too many of our brothers, uncles, cousins, and fathers had perished in that battle for the nation to ever be able to forget them. This was the battle that blood and honor helped to consecrate the hallowed grounds of Gettysburg with.

2

Maine Joins The War.

"It was never my fortune to witness a more dismal, bloody battlefield."

UNION GENERAL JOSEPH "FIGHTING JOE" HOOKER -
ANTIETAM - 1862

While the noise from the cannon fire in South Carolina could not be heard as far north as Portland, Maine, news of the war's first battle would soon arrive there. The news of the war starting was just like the weather along the east coast for most of the day. Both were dark and dreary that 12th day of April in 1861.

*****

Working in his father's small boathouse just off of busy Commercial Street, a cobblestone street that sits adjacent to Portland Harbor, seventeen year old William Barton could not help but hear the noise. Pausing from the sanding he was giving to the hull of a medium sized double mast ketch that he and his father were busy repairing, he looked out the large sliding wooden door to see what the commotion was all about. Standing there, he could see several large and excited groups of people running around at the far end of the street. The noises he was hearing came from the excitement that was generated by the screams and cries of the gathering crowd.

Looking back into the boathouse, William saw the growing noise had not caused his father to give it even a moment's notice. Slowly, and with great detail, his father continued to carefully place the tar soaked strands of hemp between the newly replaced boards in the bow of the boat he was repairing. A recent spring storm had dashed the ketch, as well as a few other boats, against several large rocks sitting in the shallow waters of the harbor. In this case, the ketch's mooring line had snapped during the high winds, causing the boat to become damaged. William's father, Jacob Barton, was a third generation boat builder in Portland. His talents for building and repairing small to medium sized boats were well-known along the coast of southern Maine. Local fishermen generally sought him out first when work was needed on their boats as they knew his work was meticulous. He had also earned a reputation as being someone who would often wait for payment to be made for the repairs he had done. Jacob had long ago learned that it often took a few good catches each season for fishermen to be able to feed their families and to then pay their bills. On almost every occasion, when a local fisherman had explained his money problems to Jacob, he had told them to take care of their families first. Because of that, they had remained loyal to the Barton family business when their boats needed repairs. Jacob's business often thrived due to the compassion he had shown to these fishermen during their difficult times. Like most people, Maine fishermen never forgot who had helped them through their difficult times.

"Pa, ya don't seem too bothered by all of this hoopin' and hollerin', does ya? What do ya think it's all about?" From near the large open door, William alternated stares at his father, and at the growing size of the excited crowd.

Still focused on his work, Jacob ignored his son's question until he had finished inserting the length of hemp he had been installing between two boards. Soon finished with that part of the task, he began wiping his hands off with a dirty cloth, one that had seen far better days. Some of the tar came off of his hands easily, but all over his fingers it had caked inside the ever present cracks and blisters that his hands always seemed to have. Both of the old man's hands were rough and calloused from years of hard work.

"Think its news about the war finally starting?"

Hearing his son's last comment caused a brief smile to cross over Jacob's face. "I'm thinking ya likely figured it out!"

Still staring down the street at the excited crowd from where he stood, William hollered over his right shoulder as he headed out to see what the excitement was all about. He didn't even bother to take off the dirty and stained smock he was wearing. "Pa, I'll only be a few minutes! I want to see what the fuss is all about. I won't be long." Several nearby merchants had also heard the commotion. Now, like William, they also walked to see what the excitement was all about.

Now seated on a small wooden stool as he finished cleaning off his hands, Jacob hadn't even looked up when his son hollered to him. He had simply nodded his head at his son's excited words. As he continued to work on cleaning the stubborn residue from his hands, he sat there slowly shaking his head from side to side. They were movements of pain and disgust as he didn't need a crowd of his neighbors, or his son, to tell him what the excitement was about. He knew the country had just plunged itself into war. "The country is falling apart," he sadly thought to himself. He also knew what to expect when his only son came back from learning what had happened. He'd hold his son off as long as he could, but he also knew it wouldn't be forever.

******

"Pa, Pa," William excitedly yelled as he raced back into the large boathouse, "do ya know what's happened?"

Back to finishing the task he had been working on when his son's excitement had first interrupted his work, Jacob continued to insert the remaining sections of tar soaked hemp between the new boards he had recently replaced in the ketch. Just as he had done before, he didn't even bother to look up at his son. This time he chose not to as he didn't want his son to see the worried look in his eyes. "From the sounds of it, and from the excitement in your voice, I'm guessing some fools have caused us to go to war against each other." Not looking up had caused him to miss the excitement, and then the look of amazement, that were present in his son's face.

"How'd ya know that, Pa? Had ya heard the news about the Confederacy attacking Fort Sumter already?"

Again pausing from his work, Jacob looked up from where he still sat on the small round wooden stool. The tone in his voice would reflect the sadness he felt in his heart as it pained him to know that his beloved country had finally fallen apart. War was not something he wanted to occur during his son's life. "Weren't hard to figure out, son. Didn't know where it had happened, but the talk of war seems to have preoccupied everyone's thinking these days. Sounds like the talk has clouded up a few of their brains as well. Fools that some of those folks in Washington are, and I guess in the South as well, I ain't surprised by the awful news ya told me. Fort Sumter, huh? Guess them South Carolina folks must have taken an exception to a federal fort sitting there in their harbor. Seems like we could have worked those differences out without having to go to war over it, but I guess I ain't surprised to hear the news. News of war saddens me greatly. The war is gonna cause some hurtful feelings across this country for many a year, I do believe. Darn fools!" Jacob shook his head again from side to side as he went back to work repairing the damage to the ketch.

Despite taking in what his father had said, and despite hearing the sadness in his father's voice, William still could not suppress his excitement. It was caused by his thoughts of sharp looking military uniforms, of guns being fired, and of medals being earned for fighting so well in battle. His young and immature thoughts, like those of others who were caught up in the news of the war, were ones that had not been logically thought out. "Pa, I'm thinking of joining up to fight against them Confederate boys! What'd think?"

Jacob had expected to hear his son say those very words, and had only been surprised by how long it had taken for them to be spoken since he had returned from learning the news that war had finally started. These were the same words that so many other mothers and fathers would hear their sons utter across the land this very day. Like so many other parents felt, they were words that now caused him great anguish. "Not now, son, the time ain't right. I know you're excited about wanting to do your part and all, but you ain't old enough yet. I ain't about to give my only son to a bunch of fools who have already shown the world they're running around like chickens with their heads cut off. I ain't giving my permission for ya to go fight in some senseless war, at least not right now I ain't. Let it play out a bit so we can see if the fools who dun started this fight can get it figured out. Hopefully they can put a peaceful end to it. If not, well . . . . well I guess we'll have to see then, won't we? Best ya get back to work for now. Enough said about this fightin' business for now."

Jacob's words had been wisely spoken, but they weren't the ones William had wanted to hear. Excited at the thought of becoming a soldier, he again tried to press the issue with his father. "Pa, I think . . . ."

Quickly, Jacob interrupted his son. "William, ya heard what I've got to say for now. For now, my words, and my position, are the only ones that matter. As I told ya, I'm not about to have my only son fight in someone else's foolish war; at least not right now I ain't. We'll take a look at it again if the war lasts, but right now we're done talking about it. Get back to work. Clear them crazy thoughts from your head for now." He had said what he had to say without raising his voice as he knew doing so would likely have pushed his son away from him. For now the matter had been put to rest, but he knew it wouldn't be long before it was raised again. Silently he prayed for a fast resolution to the insanity that had started only a few hundred miles from his home.

Moving his small stool around so he could get back to work, Jacob continued to hope for a quick end to the nation's differences. Like many other fathers across the land, both in the North and in the South, he dreaded having to face the day when he would have to give his son permission to head off to war.

The quick resolution that Jacob Barton hoped for would never come. What would come was the day he dreaded. It was a day that came far too fast.

******

While the time was not right for William to go to war, Maine, just like all of the other Northern states, heeded President Lincoln's first call for volunteers to fight against the Confederacy. From Portland to Bangor to Augusta, and across all parts of the state, men from all backgrounds quickly signed up to fight. Soon fishermen, lumberjacks, carpenters, and others would fill the 2nd Maine Volunteer Infantry Regiment. It would organize in Bangor, on May 28, 1861, and it would be the first of several

Maine regiments to join the Union cause. Thousands of other Maine men would follow them off to war in the coming years.

Other units, like the 2nd Maine Artillery Unit, the 3rd Maine Infantry Regiment, and others were being organized as quickly as possible. In August, 1862, another Maine regiment would also join the cause. That regiment would be called the 20th Maine Volunteer Infantry Regiment. The 20th Maine, like the 2nd Maine Artillery Battery, and many others from the eighty thousand plus soldiers Maine sent to war, would all fight at Gettysburg. Some would fight in one of the bloodiest fights of that great battle. That fight would take place on a small hill that for years had been called by many different names. It was a hill that the world would soon come to know as Little Round Top.

3

ALABAMA JOINS THE WAR.

"Sweet home Alabama, Where the skies are so blue, Sweet home Alabama, Lord, I'm coming home to you ..."

LYRICS TO THE SONG 'SWEET HOME ALABAMA'.

A good part of what was then the United States, including those states that had, or were in the process of seceding from the Union, had already heard the news of the fall of Fort Sumter by the following morning. For some parts of the country the news had yet to reach them. Depending on where you lived, and depending on whether your support was for either maintaining the Union or for going to war against it, the news you heard was either good or bad. For Washington, D.C., and for other parts of the North, it was bad news. Whatever kind of news it was, it was news that travelled very quickly. For those parts of the country that were removed from telegraph lines, newspapers, trains, and other means of communication, the news of war starting came to you by horseback.

******

For several minutes, the horse and its rider had moved quickly across the several large opened fields at a fast gallop as they made their way to the next farm. Their progress had only been briefly interrupted by two wide, but small natural depressions they had come across, and by three small stands of pine trees that separated the fields from each other. Now past their last obstacle, they quickly resumed their fast pace. The farmhouse was soon in sight, and only a short distance away.

Halfway across the last field, the horse's rider began his cries. "Louis! Louis Hiram Pierce! Where ya be, boy! Where is ya?"

Busy as he worked in the large red painted wooden barn on his parent's small farm, where he lived with his two brothers and younger sister, Louis Pierce paused from repairing a broken plow blade and walked outside after hearing his name being hollered out. It had been hollered out very loudly, and even from where he had stood inside the barn he could tell the tone of the voice had excitement in it. The sunny bright day was unusually warm even for an early April day in Alabama, and it caused him to shield his eyes with his right hand as he looked to see the rider approaching. He could tell from the sound of the voice that it had been his cousin, Edward Russell, who had hollered out his name, but he still shielded his eyes from the sun as he watched his favorite cousin race across one of the farm's large open fields. Watching Eddie slap the backside of his horse told him something exciting must have happened.

As Eddie brought his horse to a stop near the small stone well that sat by the side of the farmhouse, Louis was joined by his younger brother, Jesse, and their sister, Margaret. She was a bubbling and happy ten year old girl who was everyone's favorite in the family. George, the oldest of the four siblings of John and Martha Pierce, was off hunting up dinner in the woods to the south of their farm when their cousin arrived.

Eddie's mother and Louis' mother were sisters who had grown up in rural Alabama with their two older brothers. Both of their parents had passed away, and Louis' mother had inherited the family farm after her brothers had both moved further out west. The two sisters had each raised four children of their own, and had lived barely a mile apart from each other their whole lives. Like two of their sons, Eddie and Louis, they also had been nearly inseparable through life.

Twenty year old Edward Russell was a very different person in life than his younger cousin. He had been named after a distant and now deceased relative, Colonel Gilbert Christian Russell, Sr., who Russell County had been named after. He was as skilled as Louis was in fishing and in hunting, but unlike his cousin he had a need to escape the country life he had been raised in. Unlike his younger cousin, Eddie had never cared too much for book learning, believing it was a waste of time. He liked to spend his time dreaming of an easier way to make a living than by the long hours he put in each day at his family's farm.

Exhausted from his long ride that morning, Eddie stood catching his breath for a couple of minutes before lowering the wooden water bucket down into the well. The cool water he soon pulled up from the fifty foot hand dug well helped to cool him down considerably. Standing in the shade that a small stand of pine trees afforded him, he slowly brushed the dust from the fields off of his clothes. He had spent the past hour galloping across the countryside telling everyone about the news of the war starting. Now it was time to tell Louis.

"Eddie, ya look as hot as a poor coon gets after it's been chased by a pack of dogs!" Little Margaret's observation of her cousin's heated condition made both Louis and Eddie laugh loudly.

After tossing the tin drinking cup back into the wooden bucket that now sat on the edge of the well, Eddie picked up his young cousin and playfully tossed her up in the air several times. Each toss brought squeals of laughter from the young girl. Finally setting her down, he smiled back at her as he wiped his sweaty forehead with his left sleeve. "Miss Margaret, y'all are getting far too big for me to be doing that much longer! Ya gotta stop growing on me, ya hear?"

Margaret laughed with glee at her cousin's comment. "I don't rightly know how to do that, Eddie? How does one stop growing?"

Finished wiping his brow, Eddie continued to smile at his pretty young cousin as he kept on teasing her. "I don't rightly know the answer to that question, but I'll find someone who does! Miss Margaret, I need to talk to Louis for a spell. You and Jesse need to give us a few minutes, OK?"

Neither Jesse nor Margaret liked missing out on the exciting news that Eddie had obviously brought with him that morning, but both knew their place in the family. They also knew that sometimes the grown-ups had to talk by themselves. Like many other children in the South, they knew not to question their elders about adult talk as the risk of being disciplined was one they didn't care to chance. With Jesse's help, Margaret reluctantly took the reins to Eddie's horse and led him to the nearby water trough so he could cool down as well.

Waiting until his younger cousins were out of earshot, Eddie excitedly spoke to his cousin. "Louis, have ya heard about it or not?"

Having no idea what Eddie was talking about; Louis asked him what he was referring to. "Heard what, Eddie? Heard that it's too darn hot already? Heard ya made a fool of yourself at the barn dance last week? Have I heard …. ."

"About the war!"

Stunned by what he heard, Louis stood still for several moments as he quickly realized that the months and months of talk about a possible war starting against the North had finally happened. "Y'all are telling me that we really is fightin' against the Yankees? I know we's got our differences 'bout things, but goin' to war against each other don't make no sense to me. We's all part of the same country, ain't we?" For several moments, he questioned his cousin about the news of the war. It was not something he ever thought he would see happen.

As quickly as he could, but slightly embellishing on some of the details as he talked, Eddie excitedly told his cousin about the Confederate cannons firing upon Fort Sumter. "I heard the Yankees did some firing back at our shore batteries, but supposedly they didn't do too much damage. I guess our boys are better shots than their boys are, huh? Heard our boys hit that fort real hard like. Got them Union boys to surrender pretty doggone quick! Not bad, huh? First time we got to fightin' and we won, not bad, huh?"

Louis stood silent for several more moments as he processed the news Eddie had given to him. A strong supporter of the stand that the Confederate states had taken, he still wondered what breaking away from the Union would mean for the South. Quietly he pondered the answers to his many thoughts. "Have we just taken on a cause we ain't ready to fight for? How long can we fight the Union army before we go and kill all of our own men off?" These were just a couple of the many thoughts and questions that raced through his now confused mind.

"Well? Ya gonna say something about what I dun told ya, or are ya just gonna stand there as quiet as a church mouse?" Still excited by the news he had delivered, Eddie stood there with a big smile on his face as he waited to hear what Louis had to say.

Eddie's comments finally snapped Louis out of his thoughts. Soon he joined his cousin in celebrating what the South had finally done. While he too was now excited about the news he had just heard, he still was aware of the many thoughts racing through his mind. Cautiously he exchanged smiles, hugs, and even back-slaps with his older cousin over the Confederacy's initial success.

Not knowing what had excited their older brother and their cousin, but seeing the two of them hugging each other and laughing out loud, the two young children knew it had to be good news that had been shared between them. Jesse and Margaret quickly join in the fun.

******

The loud excited noises had been heard by Louis' parents as they worked alone in the corn field behind one of their barns. Putting aside their rakes and hoes, they slowly walked towards the laughter and cheers they heard. Like many Southerners, the Pierce family managed their small fifty-two acre farm by themselves. They managed fairly nicely to keep the farm running well and did so without any outside help. A few larger nearby farms that sat east of theirs, and a large plantation that sat three miles to the south, had slaves working in the fields, but none worked the land owned by the Pierce family. They could neither afford to buy or keep slaves, nor did they approve of the practice of keeping men in chains. They had struggled at times to keep the farm running, but they had managed to survive due to their own hard work.

Taking notice of his aunt and uncle as they came to see what the fuss was all about, Eddie respectfully took off his sweat stained hat before greeting them. "Morning, Auntie Martha! Morning, Uncle John! I just brought y'all some great news! We just seized Fort Sumter from the Yankees! Our cannons dun blew big holes in the fort's walls so the Yankees had no choice but to surrender. Heard they even made the Yankee captain, or whatever rank he was, take down the United States flag and put ours up on the very same flagpole. Good news, huh?"

As the news of the fall of Fort Sumter had stunned so many other folks across the land that day, the news of war breaking out was a shock to the Pierce family as well.

"You sure about this news, Edward?" As John Pierce looked at his nephew for some type of confirmation about the accuracy of the unexpected news, he also held out hope that the news had yet to be confirmed.

"It's true, Uncle John. Real true! Seen the telegraph message posted outside the very same office this morning myself. The news really got the people in town talkin' this morning! Ain't never seen anything like it, that's fer sure!"

After exchanging brief glances with his wife, John and Martha, as did their children and their nephew, knelt down on the ground close to the well. As they bowed their heads, John asked the Lord for guidance through the turbulent times he sensed would soon sweep across the country.

"Dear Lord, Please spare our fine country, and all who live here, from the horrors that a war brings with it. While we are now a divided nation, please give all of us the opportunity to prosper, and to co-exist with one another. Almighty God, we pray to you to keep our children safe from harm and illness during such a difficult time. We ask this of you not for ourselves, but for our children. Amen!"

"Amen." It was a simultaneous response that was quietly uttered by Martha and all of the children.

After helping his aunt to her feet, Eddie delivered the last piece of news he had heard. "President Davis ordered all of our Confederate states to form up some volunteers to fight against the Yankees. I'm gonna volunteer as soon as I can. Gonna help whip them Yankees, I am! Heard talk last week, even before this here fightin' begun, that some kind of outfit is gonna be formed over Fort Mitchell way real soon. I'm fixin' to join 'em. Ya gonna come with me, Louis?"

Having listened to his father's prayer, and to the news that an Alabama regiment was being put together to fight the Union army, made the news of the war starting far less exciting to Louis than it had been several minutes earlier. Anxious to support the Confederacy, but none too eager to leave the life he was living, he hesitated before answering his cousin's question.

Waiting impatiently for several moments for his cousin to answer him, Eddie repeated his question again. "Come on now! I knows ya heard me as I knows ya ain't deaf. Ya comin' with me to fight them Yankees, or not?"

Still not sure of what to do, Louis nervously answered his cousin's question. "I guess I am. I guess I . . . ." The sickening feeling in his stomach, as well as the worried looks that he now saw in his parent's faces, did not allow him to finish his sentence.

In the matter of few short weeks, Louis and Eddie, as well as many other young men from both the North and the South, would soon experience firsthand the horrors of this terrible war. Some of those young men would experience it for only a brief period of time, while others would see far too much of the senseless war. Their early thoughts of glory and medals would soon be replaced by thoughts of hoping to survive the war for just one more day.

4

ANSWERING LINCOLN'S
CALL TO ARMS.

"...we must and will harden our hearts."

UNION GENERAL WILLIAM T. SHERMAN - **1863**

The peace and tranquility that the nation enjoyed had first been broken by the fall of Fort Sumter. Other battles, and other fights, soon followed the war's first hostile act. While most politicians, as well as common folks themselves, thought the war would not last past its first summer, it soon had.

During the war's first year the two armies, vastly different from each other, continued to primarily battle against each other in many different locations across the eastern part of the nation. While the Union army, one far better trained and equipped than the upstart Confederate army, struggled in many battles during the beginning of the war, the Confederate army performed remarkably well. It performed well enough that its successes soon caused great concern to both President Abraham Lincoln and to the Union generals who opposed this confident brash new army.

Not nearly as polished or as professional or as well supplied as its foe, the Confederate army had the ability to sustain itself by living off the land far better than its counterpart could. It was also an army that was staffed by many well trained officers who had left the ranks of the Union army when war had broken out. Like the soldiers they would soon command, these officers had chosen to leave the ranks of the Union army as they could not bear to take up arms against their home states.

While the Union army often times could not get out of its own way, due to the lack of leadership from a revolving door of commanding

officers, the Confederate army often times moved very quickly. The
Union officers who initially commanded the army, especially the Army
of the Potomac, were well respected army officers, but were often
generals who quickly demonstrated they were not the aggressive leaders
their armies needed. The Confederate army routinely out marched and
outperformed their rivals. The Confederacy also had several officers,
including General Robert E. Lee, General Thomas 'Stonewall' Jackson,
and a host of others, who often got more out of their men than most
Union generals seemed to be able to do with their men. Unlike one
of the commanding generals of the Union army, General George
McClellan, the Confederate generals seemed to know when to fight, and
when not to. Defensively, and even when they took the opportunity to
take the offensive position in a particular battle, the Confederate army
outperformed the Union army in many early engagements of the war.
Despite outfitting his army with as many men, with as many horses,
and with far more material of war than the South could ever hope to
give to their army, the lack of direction, as well as the lack of leadership
in his army, greatly frustrated Lincoln.

******

By the summer of 1862 many Union soldiers were coming close to
having their ninety-day enlistments about to expire. Concerned over
the number of soldiers who would not reenlist as the war continued to
grow, Lincoln put out another call for additional volunteers. Across the
South, additional calls for volunteers were also taking place.

******

In Maine, in August, 1862, President Lincoln's call for an additional
300,000 soldiers was loudly heard. With men that ranged in age from
eighteen to forty-five, and again with men from all parts of the state,
including the Portland area, the 20th Maine would soon be born.

******

Making his way across Portland's town square after running a few
errands for his mother, William Barton stopped to read a newly posted
recruiting notice that had been tacked to the Message Board in front of
the town hall. Reading the notice, he saw that a *Call to Arms* had been

announced for a new regiment that was being formed. As he finished reading the announcement for the second time about the new regiment, one that would be called the 20th Maine Volunteer Infantry Regiment, a sense of excitement rushed through his body.

Looking at the parchment colored notice, one which had a picture of a large ferocious looking eagle spread out across the top of it, William noticed that it held a banner in its mouth. Carefully he read the wording inside the banner. *"Come join the 20th Maine!"* Studying the notice for the third time, and not wanting to miss a single printed word, he again read the wording very carefully. Some of the wording had been printed in large letters to attract the attention of young men just like him.

"Volunteers Wanted!"

Volunteers needed for Colonel Adelbert Ames' 20th Maine Volunteer Infantry Regiment. Volunteers are being raised under General Order 191 of the War Department.

A bounty of $402.00 will be paid by the United States Government.

William whistled as he read the part about the bounty being paid to volunteers who joined the regiment. The dollar figure was more money than he had ever seen. Excited now more than ever, he slowly read on.

We have the best assurances that an additional amount of $100.00 will be paid before the Volunteers leave Maine! Soldier's pay will start from each soldier's enlistment date.

The total bounty paid to each Volunteer will be $502.00!

William continued to read on, but he was so excited by the news of the new regiment being formed, and about the ungodly amount of money being paid to each soldier who joined the regiment, that he absorbed little more about what was written on the notice. The only other detail that he remembered reading as he turned to walk back to his father's boatyard was that additional information regarding the new regiment could be obtained directly from Colonel Ames himself at the end of the week at Ross' General Store. Ames would be there then signing up some of the newest members of the regiment himself.

Finished digesting the contents of the notice, William walked back down Wharf Street towards his father's boatyard. Soon entering the boathouse, he saw his father speaking with a local fisherman who needed some repairs done to one of his fishing boats. Patiently he waited until his father had concluded his business.

"About time ya got here, boy! Where ya been all this time? Checking out the pretty girls up by the Square, no doubt?" The gruff tone in his father's voice had been poorly feigned as anger.

William nervously smiled at his father's attempt at being angry with him, but he was too nervous to put much of an effort into it, or to joke back with him.

"What's wrong, boy? Ya usually laugh at my jokes! Something ailing ya?"

"Yes, sir, that there is."

First looking at his father, and then back out the door of the boathouse, William fidgeted with the cap he had had been wearing. Anxiously he waited for the conversation to continue.

William's unexpected answer caused Jacob to put down the tools he had been putting away from on top of his cluttered workbench. Walking over to where his son stood, he eyed the boy before speaking. "Ya been up to the Square again, and seen another one of them recruiting announcements, ain't ya?"

Excited on the inside, but nervous on the outside, William confirmed his father's suspicions. "Yes, sir, I have. The new one that's just been posted is calling for volunteers for a new infantry regiment. They're gonna call it the 20th Maine Volunteer Infantry Regiment. It's the regiment I need to join; it's got my lucky number all over it, Pa! I was born on the 20th, April 20th to be precise. Don't ya see, this is the one I'm supposed to fight with!" William had followed his father's orders for the past year, giving the war time to play out, and had patiently waited to see what direction it would take before again bringing up his desire to go and do his part. Now he knew it was the time to bring the issue up again.

William's comments did not evoke an immediate response from his father. Patiently he waited as his father sat down on a wooden box near a boat they had been working on. His father sat quietly there for several minutes with his head bowed down against his chest. No words were spoken between the two as William gave his father time to think.

Finally lifting his head off his chest, and then standing up, Jacob walked to where his son had patiently stood waiting to hear his father's words. "Son, are ya sure that this is what ya want to do? Have ya thought this out in your head like I asked ya to do? I know you've seen the names of the men . . . . boys they really were, who've been killed and who ain't coming back home. Killed for what, I ask ya?"

William saw the pain this discussion was again bringing to his father's face, but he knew this was something he had to try. He did not want his later years to be filled with regrets about not doing his part in the war. "Pa, I've got to do this. You and ma have taught me to stand up and do the right thing in life when I know something ain't right. Well, this is one of those times that I'm supposed to stand up! We ain't slave holders, and God knows that I'd never subject another person to that type of life, but there's another wrong that needs to be corrected here. For me, it ain't about freeing the slaves; it's about doing the right thing. This country ain't perfect, but we, I mean each state, swore an oath to be part of this here nation of ours. It ain't right that them Southern states now want to leave what we ain't finished building. Ya can't quit something each and every time ya get mad about something. It just ain't right what they done!"

William's comments caused his father to look closely at his almost grown son. "Sounds like ya are a might bit smarter than I've given ya credit for!" Still frightened by the thought of losing his son to the war, Jacob was beaming inside at the position his son had taken. He could now tell his son's motivation to fight in the war was no longer just about fancy uniforms and winning medals, but rather it was now about wanting to be a part of helping to restore peace and to restoring the Union to what it once had been. The position his son had taken was one he could not logically argue against.

"Pa, I ain't gonna go do anything crazy during my time fighting. I may not come back, but it won't be because I done something foolish. Ya got to believe me on that. Besides, I'm going off to fight with a bunch of Maine boys, some from Portland likely, we'll look out after each other. Pa, I've got to do this, and I want to know you're behind me."

Moving even closer to where his son nervously stood, Jacob first extended his right hand to his son. As they shook hands with each other, he used his left hand to draw his son closer to him. It was the first time he had displayed any real sense of affection to his son in years. "Make sure ya come back to me, hear!"

William simply nodded his head in response to his father's comment as they stood there hugging each other. The simple nod acknowledged that he had heard what his father had said to him, and that he understood the love his father had for him.

"OK, son, I've got work to be doing. Go join them Yankee soldiers, and do what ya have to do to bring the Rebs back in line. Go sign up, I understand what you need to do. We'll tell ma later over supper what you've gone and done."

******

In late August, the 20th Maine, with West Point graduate Colonel Adelbert Ames as its first commander, was mustered into military service at Camp Mason, near Portland. They were sworn into service by Maine's governor, Israel Washburn. Ames, a Maine native from Rockland, had previously served in the war, and had been wounded in the First Battle of Bull Run.

In early September, on the day they were to leave for war, each member of the regiment listened to speeches that described them as proud brave soldiers from Maine. They each had already sworn an oath to obey their orders, and to defend the Constitution of the United States, and they had each formally signed the regiment's muster roll. After the speeches had concluded, they stood in formation to be formally inspected.

Later that day as the nine hundred and sixty-five members of the 20th Maine prepared to leave from Portland's Union Station on their way to Alexandria, Virginia, William introduced his father to one of the regiment's newest officers. "Pa, this here's Colonel Chamberlain,

Lt. Colonel Joshua Chamberlain, to be precise. He's a school teacher at Bowdoin College."

After briefly speaking with each other for only a few minutes, Jacob shook hands with Colonel Chamberlain, wished him well, and then made only one simple request of him. "Colonel, I expect ya to take good care of my boy while he's with ya!" It was a request that several other fathers would also ask of Chamberlain that day.

"I'll do that, sir. I promise you I will."

******

Soon the regiment boarded trains to Boston for the first leg of their travel to Virginia. From there, it would then be on to Washington, D.C. Prior to boarding the trains, the soldiers and officers said their goodbyes to their loved ones. As it was for many of the other new soldiers, William's mother and father both were there to see their son off.

"Take care of yourself, son. I'm getting older now, likely gonna need some help in the boathouse sooner than I'd like. Gonna need ya there with me. Your mother is expecting you to make her a grandmother someday. Best ya not disappoint her!"

William understood the hidden meanings within his father's comments. "Nothing to worry about, Pa. I'm planning on coming home. I promised you I wouldn't go and do something crazy. You and I are still gonna build many more boats together. Ma's gonna have a bunch of grandbabies to watch over someday."

Jacob and his wife weakly smiled at their son's response as they tried to hold back their emotions. William's distraught mother had been crying ever since she had woken up that morning, fearing, like all mother's do, that she would never see her son again.

Kissing his mother on her cheek, William said his final goodbye as the order was given to board the train he was assigned to. "Take care of ma, Pa. I'll write you both a letter soon." Fighting back his own tears as he boarded the train, William looked back at his parents. "Don't worry about me, I'll be fine! Just take good care of each other!"

Quickly settling into his seat, William waved out the window to his parents for the last time as the train began to slowly move away from the railroad station. As he did, he thought of the last words he had said to his parents. "I hope I haven't promised them something I may not have any control over." Bowing his head as the train cleared the station, he briefly prayed. "Dear Lord, please watch over my parents while I am gone. Please, Lord, let me return safely to them when this madness is over with. Amen."

******

After arriving in Boston, the 20th Maine first travelled to Virginia on the steamer *Merrimac*. On Sunday, September 7th, they arrived late in the day in the nation's capital. Arriving there after a long march, they were less than pleased to learn that they would spend their first night camped in a littered strewn empty lot not too far from the capitol building.

The very next day would start the clock ticking to when the men of the 20th Maine would meet their destiny at Little Round Top.

5

THE FIGHTING STARTS FOR LOUIS.

"It is well that war is so terrible, otherwise we should become too fond of it."

GENERAL ROBERT E. LEE,
FREDERICKSBURG, VIRGINIA, DECEMBER, 1862

After Louis and Eddie, and the rest of the roughly nine hundred men of the 15th Regiment of the Alabama Infantry had been mustered into service on July 3, 1861, they were outfitted with their equipment. Then they were sent off to war to fight against the Yankees.

During their first few weeks of training, Louis and Eddie, both of whom had been assigned to Company G, learned as much as possible about the other companies within the regiment. The eleven companies that formed the regiment were all men from Alabama. Company 'A' of the regiment had also taken to calling themselves Cantley's Rifles. They had been named after their regimental commander, James Cantley, who had formed the company shortly after the war had broken out. In talking to other soldiers from the regiment, Louis learned that the other companies were comprised entirely of men from Barbour County, from Pike County, from Macon County, and from three other counties in the southeastern part of the state. As they learned more about the regiment each day, Eddie took to boasting that it "was the best one in the whole dang Confederate army." No one really objected to him boasting that way, but some of the more educated men in the regiment knew that many other fine fighting units existed across the South.

On their third night out of Alabama, they camped with several other regiments in a large open field that was surrounded on all four sides by a thick line of woods. While no threats existed in the area from any Union troops, the sergeants from several of the various companies put a picket line out in the woods as a training exercise for some of the men who had not been too familiar with guns. They wanted their new men to be familiar with the duty so they would be ready to assume it when necessary. Having their inexperienced men standing alone in the woods at night with a rifle for hours at a time would quickly let everyone know who could be trusted in the coming weeks to watch over them as they slept.

Like most soldiers, the chief complaints that quickly started amongst the men centered on their bellies and their feet. Sitting around a small campfire that third night out, Eddie and Louis, along with Sergeant William Johnson, a surveyor from Russell County, and Private James Lafayette, who owned a small timber business with his two brothers in Macon County, talked about what they had experienced over their first few days in the army. They each complained about the quality of the food they had been given to eat, and complained about the three long days of marching in the dust and heat as they headed for training at Pageland Field in Virginia. Of the four men, Lafayette couldn't stop complaining over how bad his feet were already hurting him. Taking off his boots, he showed the others the blisters that were now present on both of his heels.

The whining and complaining had lasted about an hour before Louis finally put an end to it. "Y'all know we're a sorry bunch, don't ya! We barely gotten going and we're already complaining about everything. What's gonna happen when the bullets start flying?" The others laughed at Louis' comment. They each quickly realized that it actually hadn't been as bad as they had made it out to be.

But just as quickly as the complaining had stopped, it quickly fired up again. As usual, Eddie spoke the loudest, and the most often, mostly about the food they had been fed that night. "I ain't sure what it all was that we got fed tonight, some kinda stew I reckon, but it sure didn't taste too good! I sure do need more food than that to keep me marchin' as I can't be doing all of that walkin' on an empty belly. No, sir!" Sgt. Johnson nodded his head in quiet support of Eddie's comments.

Sitting there barefooted, Lafayette agreed with Eddie for the most part, but being a person who truly lived off the land back home he actually thought the food had tasted good. "I thought the grub was downright good! Thought I tasted some yams and some kind of meat in that meal. Probably pork, but it mighta been possum meat also. I love the taste of a good cooked possum! I's got fed late, almost dark when I got my fill so I couldn't see what I was eatin', but it was tasty. Weren't momma's cooking, but it got the job done. I suspect we might be havin' some worst tastin' meals than that when we's out fightin' someplace."

The others gave a chuckle to Lafayette's take on the dinner meal, but Louis passed on the thought of having to eat a Possum Pie for dinner. The mere thought of having to eat a grilled possum made his stomach uneasy. "Let's hope it don't get that bad, fellas!" Taking a moment to stir the dying fire before he threw a few more dead pine branches on it, he questioned Sgt. Johnson about the many different types of muskets he had seen the members of the regiment carrying.

"Not really sure why it's that way, Louis. Likely some men brought their own muskets from home, some, like those boys in Company A, were given those Mississippi rifles, and others were given whatever smoothbore rifle that was available. Likely men got what was available when they signed up. I hear guns, just like it seems to be with money these days, are tough to get. Probably this here army is grateful to have what we got. Might have to do some scavenging on a battlefield to get something better than what we got now. Hate to take a dead man's gun from him, but if he ain't gonna use it no more then I might as well have it." The others shook their heads in agreement about picking over what had been left on a battlefield for their own needs as they realized in some cases doing so might let them live another day. As they talked, Sgt. Johnson told the men that he had heard talk of them being assigned Enfield or Springfield rifles soon, but wasn't sure when that was going to happen.

After several more minutes of army talk, the conversation changed topics. Each of the men spoke of home, and of what and whom they were going to miss the most. After spinning tales about home, the men started to drift off to their waiting bedrolls. As they did, the noise of a musket being fired in the woods off to their left was heard. Soon they heard an excited voice hollering from inside the dark tree line. "I gots me a Yankee! I shot a Yankee!"

Rushing to where the soldier on picket duty was standing, Sgt. Johnson questioned the soldier, a young nineteen year old from Pike County, on what had happened. "Sergeant, I was doing what ya told me to be doing. I was doing my picket duty when I heard a noise right over yonder." Pausing a moment, the young soldier pointed in the direction of where he had fired his musket. Doing so caused Eddie and Lafayette to head over in that direction to see what they could find. "I told him to stop, sergeant, but he dun took off on me. Had to shoot him as I couldn't think of what else to do!" While Johnson didn't utter a word after hearing the soldier's explanation over what had happened, he did stand there with a disgusted look on his face. He knew there wasn't a single Union regiment within miles of their position.

In a few minutes, Eddie and Lafayette were soon walking back to where Sgt. Johnson, Louis, and the young soldier still stood. Holding up his rather large hunting knife in his left hand as he got back to where the others all stood, Eddie continued to hold it high in the air for several moments before he wiped the blood off the blade onto his left pant leg. "Sarge, ya better get one of them cooks out here quick! This here soldier shot him alright, but he didn't kill him. I finished him off with my knife; slit his throat from side to side!"

With his eyes almost bugging out of his head, the young soldier looked at Eddie with a stare that almost made the others laugh. "Ya ain't gonna eat a dead Yankee soldier, are ya?"

"Nope! But I'm gonna eat the dang deer ya done shot, ya idiot! Darn fool can't tell the difference between a deer and a Yankee. One good thing I suppose, at least we'll know what kind of meat we's eatin' tomorrow night!" Eddie's comments caused the others to howl with laughter for several minutes. Despite his embarrassment, even the young soldier couldn't help but to laugh at his mistake.

Word quickly spread through the camp that night about what had happened, and how the 'Yankee soldier' had been gutted by Eddie. Sgt. Johnson, in telling the story to others, made many of the men laugh when he paid a compliment to the young soldier who had shot the deer. "He's a right fine shot! Just don't stand in front of the boy when he's fixin' to fire his musket as he might think y'all are another deer or, worse perhaps, another Yankee soldier!"

Needless to say, Johnson assigned his young soldier picket duty for several more nights as it was obvious that he needed some additional training in this area. Inexperienced, and far too young to be fighting in a war, this young soldier would soon be one of the 15th Alabama's first casualties.

******

Several days later, as they continued to march north, men from the 15th Alabama would begin to feel ill. One after another, the men started running fevers, began coughing frequently, and began finding small spots all over their bodies. After examining the symptoms the men all had, the few doctors travelling with the several regiments confirmed the illness to be measles. Soon over one hundred and fifty men began to fall victim to the measles.

Gathering many of the men of the 15th Alabama together on the night they had confirmed what the disease was, one of the doctors told them what it was that was causing them to feel ill. Dr. Edward Kindle, a thirty-seven year old rural physician from Macon County, who was serving as the only doctor for three different Alabama regiments, spoke to the men that evening.

"Men, y'all seem to have the measles now. We don't know too much about what causes it to break out like it has, but likely one or two of ya had the virus and now most of ya have been exposed to it. We just want ya to know the virus is gonna cause ya to start feelin' poorly. It's likely that each of ya is gonna get a rash. It's not gonna be pleasant to live with for four or five days, but for most of ya it's gonna go away. Some of ya may even have it for up to eight or nine days. If any of ya get real sick, like having a real bad case of the trots, then ya have to let one of us docs know about it. Just to play it safe and all, if ya ain't got the virus by now, stay away from the men that do have it. It's likely being spread among ya somehow, so best ya take the precaution not to be sharing the same tent with someone who's got the disease already."

After reaching Pageland, Virginia, efforts were made to get the men trained while they fought off the measles virus. Soon it was decided that due to the ongoing measles outbreak, the regiment would be transferred to Camp Toombs, Virginia. Here they could finish their training while hopefully preventing any additional exposure of the disease to any other regiments. The measles outbreak continued to severely hit the men of the 15th Alabama for several more days.

While Louis escaped the worst of the outbreak by contracting only a mild case of the measles, Eddie was hit hard. He was laid up for several days as he tried to shrug off the deadly outbreak. During this period of time several men died from the outbreak. They had died from a children's disease and not from the hands of a Yankee soldier. All of them would have preferred a more glamorous way to die.

******

As the weeks progressed into the spring of 1862, the 15th Alabama finished their training and began to move further north into Virginia. Like their Union counterparts, they had learned how to march both as a company and as a regiment, they had learned how to move in different formations, how and when to salute, how to handle and shift arms to various positions based on commands that were given, how to use their bayonets, and much more. They had learned, just as the Union soldiers had, that war would require them at times to kill an opposing soldier. Most importantly, they had also learned how to defend themselves during the brutal fighting they would encounter.

While they had trained at Camp Toombs, they had become part of General Isaac Trimble's brigade within Major General Richard Ewell's division of the Army of Northern Virginia. Then shortly after that the 15th Alabama was transferred to another division commander. Their new commander now was Major General Thomas 'Stonewall' Jackson.

******

In May, 1862, the 15th Alabama, including Louis, and his fellow soldiers of Company G, moved into the Shenandoah Valley as part of Stonewall Jackson's Valley Campaign. As the armies moved through the valley, Louis gained more and more confidence in his abilities as he had managed to survive the first few battles he had fought in.

At the Battle of Front Royal, in Warren County, Virginia, after marching for miles along muddy roads, Louis fired his first hostile shot of the war as he had been held in reserve in the other battles before now. Nervous as he fired his first shot, due to Union soldiers and their artillery brigades firing upon his regiment's position, he missed his intended target. Nervously fumbling as he reloaded his musket, he managed to finally calm himself down as he took aim at his second target. Raising his rifle, he took aim at an exposed Yankee soldier standing next to a scrub pine tree. Carefully squeezing the trigger, his second shot struck its target. "I got one! I got one! I got me a Billy Yank!"

The moment of euphoria quickly turned to guilt as Louis watched as the Union soldier writhed in pain on the ground. Struck in the upper left shoulder by the shot that had been fired at him, the young soldier struggled to get behind a nearby thick pine tree so he would not be shot again.

Despite his momentary feelings of guilt over injuring another soldier, Louis' feelings were temporary as other Union soldiers began to zero in on his somewhat exposed position. Kneeling down to minimize his chances of being shot while he reloaded his musket, Union minie balls chewed up the soft ground around him as they landed. Others stripped bark off of nearby pine trees, while other wayward shots splintered some of the nearby younger saplings when the minie balls impacted on parts of their thin tree trunks. Finished reloading, he gave a brief glance in the direction of where the soldier was that he had shot. Slumped down on the ground, almost as if he was sleeping, was the dead soldier. Forcing himself to divert his gaze away from the soldier he had shot, Louis looked for another Union target to shoot at. It was war, and at times like this he knew it was shoot or be shot. His happiness at shooting the first soldier had now quickly faded away. He would never rejoice again over shooting any Union soldiers.

Later that night, still sweating, and filthy from a long day of fighting, Louis struggled to eat his supper. Despite the efforts made by Eddie, and by other friends from his company, he could not help but to think about the soldier's life he had taken. "That poor soldier is never gonna eat another meal again. He's never gonna be able to sit around the campfire like I'm doing right now with my friends. He's never gonna be able to do anything because of what I've done to him. I've killed him!" Putting his small tin plate on the ground, his meal not finished, Louis silently prayed for forgiveness. "Please, Lord, please put an end to this insanity soon!"

Like most soldiers after they kill their first man, Louis spent several restless hours thinking about the first man he had killed. In the coming weeks, he would kill several more Union soldiers, but for the rest of his life he would never forget the first life he had taken. His dreams over the many years that followed the war would never allow that to happen.

The insanity that Louis experienced that day would not end for almost three more years. For him personally it would come to an end in just over one year.

For now, Louis would have to endure many more battles before it ended for him. Like the Battle of Front Royal, he would participate in many more Confederate victories before he would be out of the war. He would perform well in all of the battles and skirmishes he fought in, even being recognized on several occasions by his commanding officers for efforts *"above and beyond the call of duty."* Those efforts, at the First Battle of Winchester, in Frederick County, Virginia, and at the Battle of Gaine's Mill, in Hanover County, Virginia, would additionally reaffirm to him how much he hated the horrors of war. In just those two battles alone, he would see five of his closest friends in the regiment killed, and would see several more sustain serious wounds.

During this period of time, Louis did get to see several Confederate generals that he had heard so much about. In camp one late June evening, he wrote his second letter home to his parents, describing to them who he had briefly met or seen during the war.

June 23, 1863

Dear Mother and Father,

I'm writing this here letter from up in Virginia. The countryside is really pretty. I'm hungry a good part of the time, but otherwise I'm a doing fine. I hope you both are doing the same.

As I have told y'all in my last letter I sent ya, I'm a hoping this here war does not go on for much longer. Seeing peoples bodies get blown up, seeing them die, seeing others missing an arm or a leg, ain't a real pretty sight to see. None of it pleases me at all.

Our boys keep on fighting well, but life is tough for all of us in this here army. Our spirits are high because our Generals keep us that way. Last week I dun saw General Stonewall Jackson again. He even said to me 'Good Job soldier!' It made me feel right fine. Him talking to me pleased me mightily.

We keep on beating the Yankees fairly regular like so I'm a hoping the war will be dun soon. I ain't pleased about hurting them Yankee soldiers, buts I got to if I'm to stay alive in this here life.

Tell my brothers and Little Margaret I think of them as often as I kan.

Your son,

Louis Hiram Pierce

15th Alabama

PS – Don't do no worrying about me. I ain't been shot or wounded or killed yet.

******

In the coming months, Louis and his fellow soldiers from the 15th Alabama, many who were now friends of his from several southeastern counties in Alabama, would see fighting in several other campaigns. They would fight in the Northern Virginia Campaign, at stops like the Battle of Kettle Run, at the Second Battle of Manassas, and at the Battle of Chantilly. In each of these battles they did their best just to make it to the end of each day. All around them men from their regiment, and from others they fought alongside of, fell out of the war. They were killed, and many more were injured, fighting for the cause they all believed in. Most were far too young to be making the sacrifices they were making.

In September of 1862, they would also fight in General Robert E. Lee's campaign in Maryland. One of those stops would involve the bloodiest day of the war. It would also become the bloodiest day ever for any American soldiers to experience. At the Battle of Antietam, or Sharpsburg as the Confederacy liked to call it, the Confederate army squared off against Union forces that significantly outnumbered them.

During the brutal and intense fighting that took place on September 17, 1862, especially that fighting that took place in a small cornfield not far from the Poffenberger farms, the two large armies inflicted significant losses upon each other. Those losses were experienced by several Confederate regiments before the fighting was over. Much of this had occurred before most of the country had even eaten their breakfast. The deadly fighting, most of it done in bitter and intense up close exchanges of muskets being fired indiscriminately between young soldiers from the North and South, would continue there for most of the day.

The 15th Alabama would have several soldiers killed in the vicious fighting that took place. Several others would later succumb to the injuries they had sustained in battle. Three of those soldiers who would soon die from their injuries had become close friends with Louis, and one had been from his own company.

Later, as the 15th Alabama prepared to march out of Sharpsburg, they knew they had left many of their Confederate brothers dead on the battlefield that day. Far too many had died close to the narrow bridge that would come to be known as Burnside's Bridge. Many others had died at places such as Snavley's Ford, along the Harpers Ferry Road, and in several other similar locations.

In all of these battles that were fought in and around the Shenandoah Valley, the 15th Alabama would contribute to the bloody trail the Confederate army left after each battle.

******

At the battle of Fredericksburg, in December, 1862, Louis watched in awe, and in disgust, as Union soldiers crossed the Rappahannock River, and then bravely sacrificed themselves as they tried to advance on the high ground held by him and other Confederate soldiers in and around Marye's Heights. Later, days after the battle had been fought; he and his fellow soldiers learned that the Union army had suffered over 13,000 casualties in just this one battle. They would not know it at this time, but roughly seven months later it would be Confederate generals who would basically order the same senseless slaughter of their own troops as they tried to assault the high ground held by Union forces in Pennsylvania.

At the end of the first day at Fredericksburg, Louis and his fellow soldiers of the 15th Alabama, as did many other Confederate soldiers, paid compliments to the bravery displayed by so many Union soldiers that day. As they praised their brave foes, they also questioned the wisdom of the Union officers, like General Ambrose Burnside, and others, who had ordered the senseless and numerous Union charges across the open fields of fire that day.

Warming themselves by sitting around a large fire as the bitter cold wind blew across the battlefield that night, men of the 15th Alabama spoke of what they had personally witnessed that day. "I can't believe what I seen this day. Them Blue Bellies just kept coming and coming. I can't rightly figure out what them Union generals was thinking. They had to know we was up here on the high ground and all. Why da ya think them generals sacrificed their boys like that? Don't make no sense at all!" Even Eddie, who had offered this comment, and who hated Yankees more than almost anyone, shook his head at the number of dead Union soldiers he had seen on the battlefield that day.

"Don't rightly know, Eddie, I don't know." Louis paused from speaking for a moment as he pulled his thin blanket tighter against himself in an effort to ward off the bitter cold wind. "If I was one of them Union generals I would have found another way to come at us. Shoot, coming across that open field like they did just don't make no sense at all! Many a brave Yankee soldier died out there today. Likely some are injured and still alive out there even now. Cold weather is gonna finish them off tonight. They'll be frozen to death by morning, poor fellas! This is one of them days, the 13th of December I think it is, that the Yankees will be sore about if they lose the war. Between this here fight and Sharpsburg, they sure have lost a bunch of their soldiers. I bet Old Abe Lincoln, and likely a bunch of his folks, ain't too pleased by losin' all of them soldiers like they have. As many as they dun lost, I think I'd find me some new generals. The ones they got ain't workin' out too good for them right now. Good for us, I suppose."

******

On the night of December 15th, after helping to repulse days of Union attacks, Louis rested by himself for several minutes by a small fire as the battle finally came to a close. Sitting with his hat in his lap, he said a simple prayer of thanks for being able to survive the bitter struggle. *"Thank you, Lord, for blessing me with safe passage through this horrible ordeal. I am grateful for what ya have done for me."* Just as he finished his prayer, three of his fellow soldiers from the regiment walked by where he sat. They were talking loudly amongst themselves as they came by.

"Ya know, Zeb, we won this here fight, but I got to admit that I seen no quit in the fightin' spirit of them Yankees. They are a brave bunch, but they didn't get me and I'm right grateful about that!"

"Amen!" Louis softly said to himself as the three soldiers walked past him. "Amen to that!"

6

THE CSA STARTS NORTH.

"If the valley is lost, Virginia is lost . . ."

GENERAL THOMAS 'STONEWALL' JACKSON, C.S.A. – 1862

Resting in winter quarters during the first few months of 1863, both armies continued to develop strategies for their upcoming campaigns.

By early February, the South had begun to feel the effects of the Union army's presence in Virginia. For many months both large armies had foraged what they could from the Virginia countryside, and now food, shoes, grain, and other supplies needed to keep them alive were becoming scarce. It was during this time period that General Robert E. Lee began to plan for his army to invade the North, principally the areas just north of the Potomac River.

Lee's plans to invade the North were similar to those that were first presented to President Jefferson Davis by General Stonewall Jackson in 1861. At that time, Jackson had proposed striking northern cities in Maryland, and other cities like Philadelphia, as well as destroying railroads and other factories located across other parts of the north. It was Jackson's intention, as Lee was now proposing to do, to take the war to northern soil. While Jackson's well thought out plans were denied several times by Davis, Lee's similar plan was approved. Soon steps were taken to put it into motion.

In mid-May, despite the death of Stonewall Jackson at Chancellorsville, Lee finally knew he had to take the war out of Virginia so the countryside could heal itself from sustaining two armies for far too long. By doing so, he sought to accomplish at least two other goals. By crossing the Potomac River, he hoped to be able to threaten several northern cities, including Washington, D.C., and Baltimore, by the mere presence of the Army of Northern Virginia. He believed doing so might cause Lincoln to recall additional Union soldiers from the field to bolster the defenses around the northern capitol. Operating close to Washington, Lee also hoped to further impact the dwindling northern morale and support the populace had for a war that had not been going well for the Union. Moving north would also allow his troops to seek the food they needed, as well as other supplies, from the rich farmlands of Pennsylvania. At the same time, doing so would also allow Virginia planters time to plant a fresh set of crops for the year. By taking the fight north, Lee also believed that a victory there would help gain the Confederacy the recognition they were fighting for. In early June, the orders were given to move the Army of Northern Virginia north.

After a series of brilliant moves and victories, like the one at Winchester, Virginia, Lee issued orders to General Albert Jenkins, of Major General J.E.B. Stuart's Cavalry Division, to head north into Chambersburg, Pennsylvania to start obtaining much needed supplies for the army. After entering the small town, Jenkins' cavalry unit did a considerable amount of damage to Union railroads and several bridges. This helped to set the stage for Lee's entire Army of Northern Virginia to enter the Keystone state. It also was the start of Lee's plan to obtain as many supplies as he could for his army from the fertile countryside. That part of the plan would later prove to be one of the few victories the Confederacy would realize during this campaign.

As Lee's army waded through minor battles and skirmishes on their way to Pennsylvania, they were often forced to march through grueling weather conditions. The heat and humidity, coupled with the dusty road conditions that the men marched over, nearly suffocated them. As the army continued to march north, passing through places such as Culpeper, Winchester, Hagerstown, and Sharpsburg, soldiers dropped nearly everything they had been carrying. The heat and humidity, coupled with days and days of marching, and with seemingly less to eat each day, made it harder for soldiers to carry their equipment. The only real exceptions to this were their muskets, their ammunition, and their few prized personal belongings. Similar conditions also plagued the Union army as they too pushed north to confront Lee's army.

By late June, 1863, Lee's entire Army of Northern Virginia was on the move towards Pennsylvania. Soon the army, with all of its three corps, would gather to fight in a small town called Gettysburg.

******

As Lee's Confederate army moved north, so did General Joseph Hooker's Union army. As he moved with his army, Hooker grew more and more frustrated by the lack of information he was being given regarding Confederate troop movements. Soon he ordered Major General Alfred Pleasonton's cavalry to cross the Rappahannock River to scout the positions of Lee's army. As he did, three divisions of Confederate General Ewell's II Corps rested for the night near Culpeper Court House.

At Brandy Station, on June 9th, the largest cavalry battle of the war took place between Stuart's men and Pleasonton's troopers. The result was an indecisive battle to some extent, but the Union cavalry gained some much needed confidence from this fight. They had finally realized that they were fighters who were just as good as their counterparts were. Their morale and confidence quickly began to soar. Hooker had ordered General Pleasonton to destroy Stuart's cavalry, and while that was not accomplished the Union did begin to chip away at the reputation of the Confederate cavalry.

Moving ever so slowly north through Virginia, while passing through towns such as Dumfries, Poolesville, Frederick, and Littlestown, and later through several other small towns like Hanover, the Union army faced the same trying weather conditions as the Confederate soldiers were experiencing. Heat, humidity, and difficulty in dealing with heavy road dust, caused the army to slowly push forward. The dusty and dry conditions were terrible for both men and horses to endure. It was especially true for those that moved in the middle and in the rear of the regimental marches, as they often choked on the heavy dust generated by the column's front. Even the hearty men from Maine found the dusty and hot conditions, and the lack of water, difficult to endure.

As the Union army moved north through upper Virginia, and later into Maryland and Pennsylvania, they received a stroke of good fortune. It would be unknowingly handed to them by General Lee through vague orders he issued to General J.E.B. Stuart.

On June 25th, Stuart would loosely interpret orders he had received from Lee by taking his cavalry south and east of the Union army in the area of Manassas Junction. These orders were for Stuart's cavalry to ride behind the Union lines, and to then threaten Washington. In doing so, he would be out of touch with the Army of Northern Virginia for several days. It was at this time when Lee's army was crossing into Pennsylvania, and moving closer to the small town of Gettysburg. While Stuart's cavalry would fight against the Union cavalry in several small battles after he left Lee's main body of troops, and while his cavalry did seize a large number of Union supply wagons, the delays caused by these acts were crippling to the Army of Northern Virginia. It would prove to be a time when the Rebel army needed the eyes and ears of their cavalry more than ever. Stuart's absence, as well as Lee's failure to properly use other available cavalry troops for his reconnaissance needs, would prove to have tragic consequences for the Confederacy in the days that soon followed.

As Lee's army would soon face the unknown during Stuart's absence, problems also confronted the Union army during this same critical time. One problem proved to be a reoccurring one for President Abraham Lincoln to have to endure. He would not endure it much longer.

Like the commanding generals before him, Hooker had moved his army far too slow, and had fought even slower on far too many occasions to please the President of the United States. Fed up with delay after delay, and greatly irritated by the same weak excuses he had heard from Hooker's predecessors as to why the Army of the Potomac was not ready to fight, Lincoln replaced him on June 28th, 1863, with Major General George Meade.

A Pennsylvanian, and a veteran of the Second Seminole War, Meade acted quickly at first in his new assignment by ordering Brigadier General John Buford's cavalry into Pennsylvania. On June 30th, Buford's cavalry would enter Gettysburg. Soon afterwards, the First and Eleventh Corps would follow him there. Shortly after they all arrived there one of the war's most significant battles would begin. It would be one that would change the course of the war for both sides.

7

THE 20TH MAINE FIGHTS
AT FREDERICKSBURG.

". . . their isn't infantry enough in our whole army to carry those heights . . ."
UNKNOWN UNION OFFICER TO GENERAL AMBROSE
BURNSIDE DESCRIBING THE CHALLENGE OF TAKING THE
HEIGHTS AT FREDERICKSBURG – DECEMBER, 1862

By now the blue sack coats and blue trousers that the men of the 20th Maine had been issued in August were no longer new. Months of training, marching, and everyday army life had begun to show their wear on the blue colored uniform that William had longed to wear. The uniforms had become stained with sweat, and, in some cases, quite ripe, as the men carried their recently issued Enfield rifles as they learned to march, and to shoot, during the hot and humid summer months.

Now their uniforms had also became coated with a layer of road dust as they marched along the dusty hot roads towards Antietam. Like the other soldiers in this war, they also quickly learned that the less a soldier carried the better off he was. Soon the roads they marched on, just like the roads taken by so many other soldiers, became strewn with haversacks, knapsacks, heavy blankets, and with the many other items that hot sweaty soldiers did not wish to carry any longer.

Ten days after leaving Washington, D.C., William and his fellow soldiers had their first brush with war. As they marched closer to a battle that had just begun, they could hear in the distance the sound of cannon fire as it rumbled and echoed through the nearby mountains. Soon they saw their first signs of what was to come for them over the rest of the war. Marching towards the sounds of the firing cannons, they saw men wounded in the battle walking to the rear in hopes of being cared for. Soon they came across areas where the battle's beginning skirmishes had been fought. These same areas were littered with hats, coats, muskets, and, most terrifying to new soldiers, with many dead bodies. In many cases they saw how the violence of war had mangled bodies beyond recognition. Along the way they also saw trees that had been splintered and uprooted from the effects of deadly cannon fire.

As they approached the battlefield, the decision was made to hold the 20th Maine, and other regiments of the Union's Fifth Corps, in reserve as their training had yet to be completed. The men from Maine would escape having to add their blood to that which had already been spilled on the bloodiest day the war would see. While the 20th Maine would see and hear the battle as it raged, and while they would later get to see President Lincoln, the man who had called them into action, when he reviewed the troops there, they would not fight where so many other soldiers died that day. It would soon be made known that the fight at Antietam had caused the nation to lose over 22,000 of its finest men that single day. Across the country, from north to south, far too many communities lost someone to the fighting that had occurred there. It was a terribly bloody day for both sides to have endured.

Soon William Barton and the rest of the 20th Maine were on the move south, and headed for Fredericksburg.

******

On December 10th, while camping on the outside of town, near the Rappahannock River, the men soon learned they would cross the swollen river into Fredericksburg the following morning. They would do so by way of late arriving pontoon bridges. The next morning, as William and his fellow soldiers prepared to move out, the grumbling from seasoned and rookie Union soldiers soon started.

"Who's the dang fool that wants to fight in this wretched cold weather?" It was a comment that was repeated up and down the Union lines many times. That comment was soon followed by another one. It came from a veteran of several battles. Sadly, it would reflect the mood of many Union soldiers that day. "Keep your wits about you, boys! We're about to take another good lickin' from them Rebs!"

Too nervous to even think straight, William kept to himself. He had already seen the wide open flat ground they would have to cross in order to have any chance of driving the Confederate army from the heights they now occupied. Even as a young and rather inexperienced soldier he knew it wasn't going to be an easy task to accomplish. Silently he agreed with what the others were saying about the weather as the bitterly cold wind off the river seemed to blow directly into their faces from every direction.

Moving out across the pontoon bridges as the Fifth Corps artillery brigade tried in vain to hammer away at the Confederate defenses in town, the 20th Maine moved across the battlefield into position as Confederate snipers steadily picked away at the long line of blue coats they saw advancing towards them. In moments, the air was filled with all sorts of hostile projectiles that the Confederacy threw at them from every angle possible. It would not take long for the 20th Maine to take on their first casualty of the battle.

After a long day of fighting, the Union army seized the town of Fredericksburg. As the bitter fighting continued into the morning of December 13th, William tried to take in as much as he could without exposing himself to a Confederate sniper. From the area in and around the Massaponax River, up to Marye's Heights, and back to the Rappahannock River, Fredericksburg was under siege. He had never seen anything like this before, not even at Antietam.

As Union troops charged forward early in the afternoon of December 13th, William watched as Confederate artillery blew huge gaping holes in their lines. Watching as the first few lines of soldiers regrouped, and then charged forward again, he saw scores of men crumble under the withering fire laid down upon them from Confederate soldiers positioned on the heights there. Firing his musket several times to support their attempts to take the high ground, he soon saw several Union soldiers, some missing arms, others with serious head wounds, running back towards the pontoon bridges. Desperately those soldiers sought to find aid at the medical tents that had been set up on the other side of the river.

Fighting like he had never done before, William quickly lost count of how many times he had fired his musket at those soldiers sitting above him in strong defensive positions. No matter how fast he fired back at the Confederate soldiers positioned on the heights, it seemed as if his efforts did little good. Firing and reloading, he continued to watch wave after wave of Union soldiers fall dead as they tried to attack the heights, and the other locations just outside of town.

Like so many others did over the course of the battle, William silently swore at the orders that had been given by those Union generals who repeatedly called for attack after attack all along the Confederate line. He had already counted five unsuccessful Union attacks that had been sent forward to take the well-defended heights. "If I can see this ain't working, then why can't they? This is just outright murder!"

Aided by Stonewall Jackson's efforts at cutting off the other possible avenues of attack that the Union army might try to use, Lee's battle plan worked well. Now he forced General Ambrose Burnside's men to attack his most fortified position. Like the battle that would follow almost seven months later, Burnside and Lee would both tragically learn that troops who tried to storm an elevated and fortified position would have a tough task to face. Like their losses at Antietam, the Union's losses at Fredericksburg would soon be staggering in the number of men who had been killed. General Ambrose Burnside's failed tactics would lead to more Union deaths than the army had experienced barely three months earlier.

As he took in all that was occurring, William saw Colonel Chamberlain moving in and around the men as he tried to calm them down. Confederate canister fire, and other ordinance fire, seemed oblivious to him as he talked to the men. "That is a brave man," he thought as he watched Chamberlain walk among his men as the firing from the Confederate side of the battle seemed to intensify.

"Keep your heads down, men! Don't try to be a hero today! Too many have already died trying!" Chamberlain's words and actions helped comfort William as he tried not to be either a hero or another statistic in the regimental record of the battle.

Soon word spread that they would have to spend the night camped on the field as it was too dangerous to try and withdraw the regiment from the field at this time. Trying to do so, under the watchful eyes of Confederate snipers, and artillery batteries stationed on the heights, would have only increased the body count even higher than it already was. The already cold day quickly became even colder that night as the bitterly cold wind soon dropped the temperature a few more degrees with each passing hour. Forced to do whatever they could to keep warm, the men of the 20th Maine pulled the dead bodies of their fellow soldiers closer to them. Across the battlefield, other soldiers did the same. The bodies would help to serve as windbreaks from the bitter wind, and would also serve as protection from the bullets that were constantly being fired at them by Confederate soldiers. As the night progressed, and with little clothing to help ward off the cold night, William and his fellow soldiers began to peel layers of clothing off the Union dead to help stay warm.

Shivering as he tried to stay warm, the dead bodies of several Union soldiers doing little to keep him from freezing, William hollered to a friend of his that was huddled nearby. "Herbert, I'm from Maine, just as you are, but I don't know if I've ever been this cold before. I know I ain't ever been this scared before!"

Not hearing any response from his friend, William looked to see if he was still alive. Protected by the remains of several dead Union soldiers who were stacked around him like stones in a wall, and hunkered down under three Union coats whose owners no longer needed them, Herbert was fast asleep. What he saw his friend doing was another in a long list of sights that he had never seen or experienced in life before. Too cold, and also too scared, William would not sleep much that night.

******

The following evening, after another long and cold day on the Fredericksburg battlefield, one that saw bullets and other ordinance landing around them for most of the time they were there, the 20th Maine retreated back to the relative safety of town. They had been part of the many unsuccessful attempts to dislodge the Confederate soldiers from their positions of strength. Like the other Union regiments that had fought alongside of them all day, they also had nothing to show for their efforts except the dead they stepped over as they fell back. Union morale now began to sink to one of its lowest points in the war. Desertions would soon begin to rise.

******

As war was not difficult enough to contend with, the men of the 20th Maine, like so many other soldiers on both sides, had to cope with so many other issues in their daily life while in the army. Food was often in limited supply or of poor quality; the days were either too long and too hot, or too long and too cold. Clothing and footwear was scarce at times, and their feet generally hurt from marching for miles and miles. The conditions most soldiers lived through during the war were often less than ideal. If those issues were not enough to already contend with, the 20th Maine was then saddled with another serious issue they would have to deal with. Just like so many folks living back at home, both before and after the war, the soldiers from Maine began to contract the deadly smallpox virus.

Everywhere in the regiment men broke out with the obvious signs and symptoms of the smallpox virus. It seemed as if almost everyone suffered from a high fever, terrible headaches, and, most notably, the ugly skin blisters that covered large portions of their bodies. Everyone was run down and weak from the virus they had contracted, one that may have been accidently given to them by way of a faulty vaccine.

During the outbreak, Dr. Brooks Titcomb, one of several Fifth Corps regimental surgeons, was kept busy caring for the men who had fallen victim to the smallpox outbreak. Soon he would have one more patient to care for.

From where he sat outside his small tent, William saw Doc Titcomb leave a nearby tent. Quickly he called out to him for help. "Doc, I'm feelin' somewhat poorly all of a sudden, seems like I'm running a fever just like many of the boys are doing. I got a couple of sores inside my mouth and some kinda rash on my face; got it on parts of my belly also. Do I have the smallpox illness, or do I just have the chickenpox?"

"Wouldn't surprise me if you have the smallpox, seems like it's breaking out all over our camp." Titcomb had his newest patient sit down on a small wooden chair outside a nearby tent. Quickly he began to give his patient a quick look-see. "Take your boots and socks off so I can look at the bottom of your feet, William."

Feeling too poorly to ask Doc Titcomb why he had to take his boots off, William complied with the request.

After studying the bottom of William's feet for a few moments, Titcomb gave his patient his diagnosis. "Well, it ain't chickenpox ya got, William, its smallpox. You have the telltale signs of smallpox on the bottom of your feet. For some reason, chickenpox does not affect the soles of ones feet, or the palms of hands like smallpox does."

Now somewhat scared, William nervously put his boots and socks back on. He then asked Titcomb the same question many others had already asked him. "Doc, how bad do I have it? Am I gonna die?"

Looking again at William's face and belly, Titcomb's words gave his patient some hope. "What I'm seeing doesn't look as bad as some of the other cases I've seen, seems like you've got a relatively minor case, William. This darn disease is very contagious; likely it's being spread around the camp by all of you living in the same cramped tents with each other. It may possibly be spreading amongst you from sleeping on the same cots and blankets at times as well. Some of you may be getting it from drinking out of the same drinking cups; best you not do that for a while. You might want to think about boiling your mess cup in some water before you drink out of it if someone else might have used it recently. Not sure if it will help to do this, but you might want to think about doing so just to play it safe. No real tellin' how this disease is spread. Your fever should go away soon. If you aren't dead in a week or so, you'll be fine!"

Despite being hot, fatigued, and sweating from the disease he had contracted, William's spirits were now higher than they had been due to Titcomb's favorable diagnosis. He even managed a weak laugh at the doc's last comment about dying.

Several 20th Maine men would not be as lucky as William was. During this outbreak, and in other outbreaks during the war, others would succumb to more severe cases of smallpox. The terrible disease would show no allegiance to the color of the uniforms the soldiers would wear. It would take the lives of many soldiers from both sides of the war.

******

As the 20th Maine dealt with the regular problems associated with fighting a war, and dealt with a significant number of their men falling victim to the smallpox virus that had broken out amongst them, they did so while quarantined at a location so aptly named for such diseases. It was during their time at Quarantine Hill that LTC Joshua Chamberlain was promoted to full colonel. Upon his promotion he took command of the regiment.

One of Chamberlain's first official duties as a full colonel was hardly a glamorous assignment. With his men still fighting off the smallpox disease in the area of Chancellorsville, he, along with some of his healthier men, was assigned the task of protecting the Union's telegraph lines so communications could be maintained with Lincoln, and with the War Department in Washington, D.C.

For William, who had been diagnosed with a minor case of smallpox, one known as *variola minor*, he soon recovered nicely. The majority of the 20th Maine also soon began to recover from their cases of smallpox over the next few weeks. As they did, they hoped the future held more glorious assignments for them than protecting the Union lines of communication. They had all signed up to fight in the war, not to sit and guard wires that were suspended in the air, no matter how important the wires were. They were ready to see some more action.

Very soon they would be involved in one of the most intense struggles of the war. It would be a battle that would cement their reputation, and the reputation of their colonel, as one of the bravest fighting units in the Civil War. This fighting would take place in a quiet little Pennsylvania town near that state's southern border.

8

DESERTION.

"Gordon instantly assumed the finest attitude of a soldier. He wheeled his horse, touching him gently with the spur, so that the animal slightly reared, and as he wheeled, horse and rider made one motion, the horse's head swung down with a graceful bow, and General Gordon dropped his sword point to his toe in salutation."

GENERAL JOSHUA CHAMBERLAIN DESCRIBING CONFEDERATE
GENERAL JOHN GORDON'S REACTION TO THE UNION
SALUTE AT APPOMATTOX COURT HOUSE.

The early days of June, 1863, had been long trying ones for General Joseph Hooker as he started the Army of the Potomac on its move north towards Pennsylvania. He had spent many hours planning the army's movements, spent hours conferring with his commanders, and had spent a large amount of time reading the constant flow of telegrams from the War Department in Washington, D.C. Like the rest of his army, he had been on the move for several days, sleeping little and eating less. He was a tired man, one with far too many responsibilities and far too little time to get them all done.

As the evening of June 16th came to a close, in the light provided by a small candle and one solitary gas lamp, Hooker sat in his tent finishing some overdue correspondence. Finally finished, he sealed the three envelopes up that contained the correspondence and laid them down on his small wooden folding desk so that his aide could send them out the following morning. As he sat in his rocking chair reflecting on the day's proceedings, and trying at the same time to predict what the next day would bring, his aide, Major Kent Wilson, quietly pulled back one of the flaps and entered the large tent.

Deep in thought, Hooker, at first, did not see his longtime friend enter. It wasn't until Wilson softly shuffled some of the papers he was carrying that the general realized his aide had been standing there. Despite their close relationship, Wilson never ventured far into the tent until he had been motioned to do so. It was done out of respect for both his friend, and for the position Hooker held.

As he stood there, Wilson debated to himself over whether he should have bothered Hooker so late in the evening, but quickly realized he really had no choice. "Best we get working on this tonight, I guess." Despite his presence being acknowledged, he stood there for a few more moments as he contemplated the unpleasant news he had for Hooker.

Somewhat disturbed over being interrupted so late in the day, Hooker placed the small pewter cup he had been drinking from down on his desk, and quickly sought to make this latest interruption as brief as possible. After being awake for almost eighteen hours, he was looking forward to getting into his waiting cot so he could grab a few hours of sleep before being woken to face another equally long and trying day. "Yes, Major, what is it? I hope it's at least something important given the hour of the day. I'm about ready to turn in for the night."

"Yes, sir, I'm sorry to bother you about this, but I believe we should take care of this matter as soon as possible, seeing that it's going to be an unpleasant one to deal with. If you just sign off on these papers, I will see to the rest of the details. I think we should take care of this as early as we can, possibly even tomorrow. We still have a long way to travel during the next several days, its best we get this over with as soon as we can."

"What new and unpleasant task could that possibly be, Major?" Even in the dimly lit tent, Hooker could tell that whatever the unpleasant news was, it was enough of a problem to bring a frown to Wilson's usually cheerful face.

"Sir, I'm sorry to tell you that this bad news involves three of our men. As you know, the provost marshal recently arrested these men after they were finally located last month. Each of these soldiers had deserted the army this past December. Well . . . . well, to get to the point, sir, they each have recently been court-martialed for their acts of desertion in the face of the enemy. For one of them, a young private from New

York, it's the second time he deserted the field during an engagement, and overall it's the third time he's deserted his company. For the other two soldiers it's their first act of desertion. We are . . . . "

Interrupting his aide as he briefly stood up to take another drink of water, Hooker looked at Wilson with a large frown on his face. "I'm guessing you're going tell me that they want us to shoot this boy from New York, right?" Hooker got the answer to his question before Wilson even spoke as his aide's face told him what he wanted to know.

"Yes, sir, afraid so. The court has ordered the other two soldiers to serve out the rest of the war in a military prison just out of Washington – they will be on their way there tomorrow. I've already seen to that part of the task. Seems like the court wants to make an example of these three men so others don't try to desert us along the way." Pausing a brief second, Wilson then spoke much more forcefully, and more sarcastically, than he had moments ago. "Good luck to both of them! The rotten scoundrels they each are!"

Hooker gave a weak smile to Wilson's description of the deserters who had run away from their regiments during a time of need. The smile wasn't because the men had been found guilty, but rather it was over the description Wilson had used in describing the two men's cowardice. Like his aide, he also had little tolerance for men who abandoned their posts during a fight.

"So what's the issuing facing us with the third soldier, Major?" Hooker already knew the obvious answer to his question, but wanted to hear what the court had decided upon for a fitting punishment.

"Sir, the private from New York has been ordered to be executed by Captain Eric Geier. He was the Judge Advocate at the soldier's trial. Seems like the other four members of the military tribunal, or court-martial, or whatever it's rightly called these days, also voted to execute the soldier. Like I said, they want this boy to be made an example of. The Judge Advocate's office has got a few other pending cases that are similar to this one, seems they are taking these matters right serious like, just like they oughta be doing."

Quiet for a few moments, Hooker stood there digesting the news he had been given. "I know Geier, he's a fair man. I'm sure this soldier received a fair trial." Quiet again for a few more moments, the general then asked his aide his next question. "What's the soldier's name?"

Looking down at the paperwork he still held in his right hand, Wilson searched for the soldier's name for a moment before finding it. "Private Lesley Brown, he's nineteen years old. He's from General Slocum's Twelfth Corp's First Brigade; seems he was assigned to Company F of the 156th New York."

"Far too young to be fighting in a war, and far too young to have this kind of a problem hanging over his head!" Hooker's already long day now began to grow even longer, and more unpleasant.

"General, from looking over the paperwork that's been sent to us, it all looks to be in order. The other members of the Chain of Command have already signed off on it. The paperwork just needs your signature now, and the date that you want the execution to be held on. Thought you might want to take care of signing this tonight so I can know when you want this unpleasant task to be taken care of. Like I said, if you just sign it, I'll see to the rest of the details."

Sitting back down at his small desk, Hooker looked over the paperwork that Wilson had handed to him and saw the names of the other officers who had endorsed the court's order. Picking up the quill he had been using to finish his correspondence with a few minutes ago, the Commanding General of the Army of the Potomac quickly signed his name to the order as well. "Darn messy business this is, Kent, too messy! Needs to be done, no doubt about that, but I hate this part of the war more than anything. I want it done the day after tomorrow. Have it done early in the morning, no sense making the boy wait all day for this to happen, that ain't fair to him. See to the other details, and see that it gets done right! I want some of the Corps commanders, as well as their regimental commanders, making sure their men witness this. I want this to prevent others from deserting us in the future, or to at least make them realize what the penalty is for doing so. We're going to have a big fight on our hands sometime very soon, and we're going to need all of the boys there. We can't afford to have any more of them deserting us now."

A quiet existed in Hooker's tent for several moments as the two men thought about the unpleasant task that awaited them. As they stood there, and without possibly knowing what the other was thinking, they each reflected back on the executions they had previously witnessed. Hooker soon broke their silence. "Major, make sure the boy's company commander knows about the execution as soon as possible. I don't want any of the boy's fellow soldiers being part of the firing squad. That's not the right thing to be doing. Have some other soldiers from another regiment take care of that part of the detail."

Turning to leave so Hooker could get some sleep, and so he could see to the other details of the execution, Wilson started walking to the tent's opening. As he did, Hooker called to him one last time.

"Major, make sure you find out what the boy's faith is. Get one of our chaplains over there to be with him. The boy needs someone to help prepare him for his next life. That's the least we can do for him."

As he turned to leave, Wilson heard Hooker mutter softly to himself. "God have mercy on that poor boy, and on us."

******

Like the rest of the soldiers from the 20th Maine, and like the others who had been ordered to witness the execution of Private Brown, William had stacked his rifle in one of the groups of rifles off to the side of the large field where the execution was to take place.

William and the others had just gotten into position, under the already hot sweltering sun, when the wagon carrying the prisoner, and his three armed provost guards, arrived on the field. Now they watched as the handcuffed soldier was walked several feet away from the wagon. Standing there by himself as he waited for Brown to be brought to him was Monsignor Jeffrey Hanson. He was a well-liked thirty-two year old member of the Catholic Church who often travelled with the Fifth Corps. A native of Springfield, Massachusetts, he had volunteered to be with Brown on this fateful day.

As he reached the spot where Monsignor Hanson stood waiting for him, Brown knelt down on the grass as several hundred Union soldiers stood in formation quietly nearby. Standing for a few minutes as he said a brief prayer, Hanson then knelt down next to the prisoner. From where they stood, the soldiers watched as the monsignor opened a small

Bible, and then quietly read from it for a few minutes. They watched with great interest as the monsignor made the sign of the cross as he closed the book. Several of the soldiers standing in formation soon did the same out of respect to their faith, and to the prayers that Monsignor Hanson had quietly spoken. Then standing up, Hanson gently patted the top of Brown's head as a way to additionally comfort the condemned young soldier.

From where he stood with the others, William could not help but notice that the prisoner had knelt the entire time with his eyes closed, and that he had held his head bowed with his chin pressed tightly against his chest. To him, it seemed as if Brown was oblivious to everyone else around him.

After seeing that Hanson had finished praying with the prisoner, Harlow softly whispered to William, asking him to explain what had just taken place. Harlow had never been much of a churchgoer in life.

"The good monsignor was giving Brown absolution for his sins. It's part of the sacrament of penance."

Confused by what he heard, Harlow quietly asked his friend for a simpler explanation.

"The monsignor was forgiving him for his sins so he could get into heaven. It's a place you ain't ever gonna see!" William quietly smirked at the last part of the explanation he had given to Harlow.

******

As the guards helped Brown to his feet, William, without taking his eyes off either the young prisoner or Monsignor Hanson, whispered softly to his friend. "Harlow, what's this boy really gone and done to get himself shot here today?"

"Heard he deserted his company for the third time. Also heard he did it running from the field when we were fighting alongside his boys last December. If that's true, then he deserves what he is gettin'! Ya don't run out like that when fightin' is goin' on, it ain't right to do that!"

"Guess so, Harlow. Still too bad for him as it don't seem right we're shootin' our own, but I guess you're right 'bout what ya said 'bout a soldier runnin' off. A soldier's got to do his duty no matter how scared he gets, it's that simple."

Now watching as seven soldiers marched into position roughly ten steps in front of Brown, William then saw Monsignor Hanson move closer to the condemned prisoner. Watching as a few last words were exchanged between the two men, he then saw Hanson move off to the side near a freshly dug grave.

As the sergeant who was in charge of the detail walked over to where Brown stood, William saw for the first time that a small white-colored sign had been suspended around the prisoner's neck with a piece of thin twine. The crudely made sign hung loosely against Brown's chest. It only had one word written on it. The single word identified Brown's misdeed to all who stood there that day. Painted in large black letters was the word 'Deserter'. After speaking with the prisoner for a moment, the sergeant removed the small sign and tossed it off to the side.

As a black bandana was placed over Brown's eyes, Harlow again whispered to his friend. "I heard these seven here soldiers were picked random like cause no one wants this kinda duty. Them are the boys that are gonna shoot this soldier dead. Also heard that some of their muskets have blanks in them, that way no one knows who actually fired a shot to kill the boy. Seems I heard that only three or four of them have real bullets in their muskets. Sounds like a fair way of doin' it, I suppose."

William nodded at Harlow's comments as he watched a piece of white cloth being pinned directly over the prisoner's heart.

"I guess they want to make sure those boys know where to aim, huh?" Harlow's statement did not evoke a response from William as he was too busy scanning the faces of the large crowd to see what those present were watching at the moment. To him, it seemed as if all sets of eyes were now focused solely on the prisoner, and on the white piece of cloth that was pinned to his shirt. There wasn't a murmur to be heard across the large open field.

Finished with his tasks, the sergeant walked towards the soldiers who comprised the firing squad, and then took a position immediately to their left. Standing off to his side was Provost Marshal Arnie Kinsler. Now Kinsler read the formal charges that Brown had been found guilty of. As he did, the eyes of everyone present shifted between him and the condemned prisoner. Soon finished with his reading, the only other sounds that were heard for moments were the noises that several nearby horses made. It was remarkably quiet while everyone waited for the next order to be given.

Before any formal orders were given to the firing squad, William heard Kinsler loudly ask Brown if he had any last words to say. Quickly all eyes shifted from the Provost Marshal to his prisoner. Somberly, but without showing any real emotion, Brown quietly declined the opportunity to speak.

As he saw the prisoner shake his head to decline Kinsler's offer of any last words, William could not get over how calm Brown was. Silently he thought to himself, "If it was me, I know I couldn't be as brave as that man is being right now."

William's stares at the prisoner were quickly broken by a young Union drummer boy who briefly sounded his drum. It was a signal to the firing squad to be ready for the next command. Then seeing the sergeant nod his head at him, the young drummer beat a steady beat on his drum for almost fifteen seconds. It was the loudest noise on the field as yet.

Then William heard the Provost Marshal give his first command. It was one that was given in a very authoritative tone.

"*Ready!*"

It was followed in a matter of moments by the second command of "*Aim!*" Quickly seven rifles were raised, their hammers being cocked back at the same time.

Without a warning, and without another moment of hesitation, the next order was quickly given.

"*Fire!*"

Quickly powder burned in the seven muskets, and three bullets raced towards the white piece of cloth affixed to Brown's shirt.

As the muskets fired, several soldiers standing in the formation could be seen slightly ducking when they heard the distinct noise of muskets firing. It was a noise they now associated with danger. Their reaction to the muskets firing had been an automatic reflex action they had learned from having fought in too many battles. Despite their reactions, none of them took their eyes off of Brown. Almost immediately after the muskets had fired, the prisoner fell dead. He came to rest on his back, and did so only a few feet from where he was to be buried.

"Dismissed! Fall back into position with your regiments!"

******

Retrieving their muskets, William and Harlow walked back with some of their friends from the company to join up with the other members of the regiment. They were being staged near the rear of the large field before the order was given to move out for the day. As they walked, William looked back over his right shoulder at where Brown had fallen. Now he saw two soldiers dragging the prisoner's lifeless body towards the freshly dug grave. Seeing this caused him to quickly turn his head away. He had already seen more than he wanted to see that day.

Quiet for several moments as they slowly made their way across the field, Harlow broke the silence first. "William, I don't know about you, but I ain't never once thought about deserting my regiment. Seeing what I dun seen here today, I now know I never will. I'd rather be killed by some Johnny than face down a firing squad of our own boys, that's for darn sure!"

As Harlow had spoken to him, William had been thinking about what he had seen that morning, and had also been thinking of how scared he had been at Fredericksburg when they had fought there. Quiet for a few more moments as he finished his thoughts, he realized that brutal fights like Fredericksburg could easily cause a soldier to desert his post. He hoped he never would get that scared. "I hear ya, Harlow. I hear ya."

******

As the two large armies marched independently of each other towards their meeting in Pennsylvania, desertion was an issue that was always on the minds of officers from both sides of the war. During the fighting that would soon take place in Gettysburg, soldiers from each of the two armies would desert their posts in times of need. This would be especially true for the Confederacy during their retreat south after the three days of intense fighting in Gettysburg. Many would leave the Confederate army as they saw hope dwindling for their cause. Others simply left so they could get back to their farms to help with the crops that needed tending.

For William, and the many other Union soldiers who had witnessed Brown's execution, life in the army was already too tough to endure at times. They didn't dare to add to their problems by thinking about deserting, or to wonder who it would be that would come after them if they had deserted. Just like his friend, William did not care to share a fate similar to Private Brown's. The mere thought of being executed by their fellow soldiers kept William and Harlow from even remotely thinking about deserting.

9

THE HILL.

"I have been tried and condemned."

UNION GENERAL GEORGE MEADE AFTER BEING APPOINTED
COMMANDER OF THE ARMY OF THE POTOMAC.

On June 30th, as General Buford's cavalry had ridden into Gettysburg, so had the soldiers who were assigned to Confederate General A.P. Hill's Corp. Earlier as he reached the area in and around the small town of Cashtown, Pennsylvania, located slightly to the west of Gettysburg, Hill found that Union troops had already entered the small town. Soon other Confederate troops would follow Hill's Corps there.

Despite Lee's desire not to fight a significant battle on their first day in Gettysburg, as all of his Corps had not yet arrived, a fight was unavoidable as both armies began to jockey for position. Soon a fight erupted between General Richard Ewell's soldiers and Union troops. Fighting raged through the afternoon, with both sides having the advantage at times, but the late arriving troops of General Jubal Early helped to carry the day for the Confederacy as Lee's army pushed the Union troops back through the streets of the small northern town.

Neither army knew what to expect after that first day, but both knew the days that followed would be ones that would be far worse than what they had already experienced. Whatever was about to come would follow on the heels of the Confederate victory that first day.

******

The two hills that lay to the south of the Union line were areas that neither General George Meade or General Robert E. Lee had given much thought to as they prepared their armies to fight on Day Two. Strategically, at first, neither hill was thought to mean too much to either side.

At the far end of the Union line, Little Round Top sits adjacent to the larger hill known as Round Top. Little Round Top rises only a few hundred feet above the small valley that separates it from Round Top, and rises a similar height from Plum Run, which sits between its base and Devil's Den. On most days reaching the crest of Little Round Top is a fairly easy task to complete, even when factoring in the steepness of the hill's slopes, and the ancient boulders that are strewn about the area. But July 2nd, 1863, was not one of these typical ordinary days.

******

During the morning of Day Two, from the northern most point of his line at Culp's Hill to Little Round Top, situated near the southern end of the Union line, Meade carefully laid out his corps of men into the positions he wanted them to assume. He placed them in the shape of an inverted fishhook in anticipation of what Lee was about to throw at him. He knew doing so would also allow him to replenish his line quite easily when needed during the day.

If Meade's line of defense had been adhered to like he had laid it out, with General Daniel Sickles' Federal Third Corps manning the smaller of the two hills, then the name of Little Round Top might not have ever been added to the long list of well-known battlefield locations at Gettysburg. But Sickles ignored Meade's order of where to place his Corps, and moved his men far out in front of the rest of the Union line, placing them close to the Emmitsburg Road. By doing so, Sickles not only exposed both of his flanks to being attacked quite easily, but also left his Corps in a vulnerable location far out in front of the rest of the Union line. Resupplying Third Corps with reinforcements, and also having to cover the hill he had left exposed, would burden the Union army late that afternoon.

While neither Round Top nor its smaller neighbor, Little Round Top, received little attention from Meade, and others, until fighting had started there late in the afternoon on July 2nd, it had also received little attention from Lee, General James Longstreet, and General John Bell Hood. The intelligence that these Confederate generals had been given clearly implied that the left flank of the Union army did not extend as far south as Little Round Top. It would not be a position that received anyone's attention until the Confederate attack pressed forward towards Devil's Den. It was only then that both sides realized the hill had been left unguarded.

Acting on orders from Meade, Brigadier General Gouverneur Warren, while inspecting the advanced forward position that Sickles had taken, noticed Confederate movements were taking place close to Little Round Top. It was due to his observations, and due to his realization of how the Union line could possibly be turned if the Confederate troops had taken either of the two hills, that Union troops were quickly moved to the top of Little Round Top by Colonel Strong Vincent. Vincent's deployment of the 20th Maine, along with several other regiments, including six guns from Lt. Charles Hazlett's Fifth Corps artillery brigade, were soon put in place to defend Little Round Top. They arrived only moments before the Confederate attack began.

******

As Lee pressed for the Confederate attack to move forward through the area of Devil's Den late that afternoon, neither General James Longstreet or General John Bell Hood favored moving through, or fighting over, terrain that was strewn with large and ancient boulders. The terrain that their men would have to cross over would put them at a distinct disadvantage. Longstreet tried repeatedly to convince Lee that the best plan was to skirt the two hills and to come up from behind the Union lines by way of Round Top. Despite his repeated attempts to convince Lee to alter his plan, he refused to do so. Lee's failure to listen to one of his most trusted generals, as well as the late arriving Union soldiers that were being deployed along the crest of Little Round Top, would cause the day to be one that the Confederacy would soon regret.

As the fighting began on the right flank of the Confederate line, Colonel William C. Oates pressed forward with his soldiers from the

15th Alabama. Soon chaos and confusion appeared in the advancing Confederate line. It had partially been caused by the rough boulder strewn terrain that broke up their advance towards Devil's Den. This problem quickly caused Oates to advance further south of where he had been directed to move. Advancing up the slope of Round Top, he quickly realized the advantage that holding such a position would give to the Confederacy. However, his thoughts of moving troops and artillery to the top of the hill, as well as clearing fields of fire for the cannons so they could strike the exposed left flank of the Union line, were soon dashed by Captain Leigh Terrell, General Evander Law's adjutant. Terrell quickly ordered him to attack the Union lines as he had been directed. From his position on Round Top, Oates knew that attacking up the exposed steep slopes of Little Round Top would mean exposing his troops to the view of Union soldiers.

Before moving out to follow his orders, an exasperated Oates moaned out loud rather loudly, "Does anyone besides me see the prize we have already taken? We can attack the Union left from this very spot, and damage the Yankees plans significantly! It will save the lives of many of my men!" It was out of pure frustration that Oates had asked this to no one in particular as he also believed the hill could easily be defended by a small group of soldiers while artillery units fired away at nearby Union positions.

Quickly obeying the order he had been given, Oates moved his men down the north slope of Round Top to attack the soldiers of the 20th Maine. He would soon lose many of his soldiers as he had predicted. His predictions and concerns had also been the same predictions that Longstreet and Hood before him had raised with Lee. As the Alabamians moved closer to the Union line, the first angry exchange of musket fire occurred between the two lines. Oates would later claim that the first volley fired at his men was among the most destructive he had ever seen. Moments after being pummeled by the first round of hot lead being fired at them from the 20th Maine, the 15th Alabama and 47th Alabama would be hit with another devastating volley, this one fired at them by the 83rd Pennsylvania.

Early in the fighting, Oates would see Captain James Ellison of Company C fall dead. Soon afterwards, Company G would also lose, in fairly rapid succession, two of their commanders. Captain Henry Brainard, and Lt. John Oates, both would be shot dead attacking Union positions along Little Round Top. The death of his brother would haunt Colonel Oates for years.

******

By the end of the day, in a fight that lasted a few short hours, eleven Confederate brigades would meet twenty-two Union brigades head on. They would fight in places such as Devil's Den, the Wheatfield, the Peach Orchard, on Little Round Top, and in at least five other places in and around the southern spur of Little Round Top. They were places that soon would be part of the lexicon of Gettysburg, and of the war itself. The fighting in those areas would cost both armies a total of 15,000 casualties. Among the Union casualties would be many of their most experienced officers. A thirty-four year old colonel from Maine, one assigned by Vincent to defend the extreme left flank of the Union line that day, would be one of the few Union officers to leave the battle alive. Remarkably, so would Colonel William C. Oates, his principle adversary that day. By the conclusion of this one brutal fight alone, the 20th Maine would lose one hundred and eighty-six of their men.

For being, at best, an afterthought in the plans of both Meade and Lee, this small hill would play a significant role in deciding the outcome of the fighting at Gettysburg.

Late June – Early July, 1863

10

MARCHING AND MORE MARCHING.

"The enemy is there, and I will strike him there!"

GENERAL ROBERT E. LEE TO GENERAL JAMES LONGSTREET –
GETTYSBURG – JULY, 1863

Like many large armies, confusion and miscommunication was often present within the Confederate army, and on the days of June 30 and July 1, 1863 it was no different. In fact, it had intensified, and it had taken shape in many forms. Those conditions, as well as the roads in and around the Pennsylvania border close to Gettysburg, jammed with huge numbers of men, wagons, horses, cannons, and the other accouterments of war, ground the Confederate advance to a slow halt. At times, some Divisions, like those of Generals Lafayette McLaws and John Bell Hood, had to wait until other Corps and Divisions cleared the roads before they could advance to their positions north of the border.

With the roads full of traffic, Brigadier General Evander Laws' brigade moved out towards New Guilford to head off Union troop movements in that area of Pennsylvania.

As they marched along the dusty road towards New Guilford, Eddie and Louis spent time talking about the changes they had seen since they joined the army. "Ya know, Louis, I sure can't figure out how things do work in this here army. I mean, we dun started the war with Ol' Jim Cantley as our commander, then we's got moved under the command of Stonewall Jackson himself, and now we is part of General Longstreet's First Corps. Heck, we even got us a fairly new colonel as the head of this regiment. Gots us Billy Oates! A down home country boy from Alabama is running this here show for us! It sure is rightly confusin' and all, ain't it?"

Wiping the sweat from his dirty face with the right sleeve of his equally dirty shirt, Louis kept an eye out for Union snipers in the woods as they marched along. As they had marched throughout the day, he had picked up pieces of scuttlebutt from other soldiers about a big fight being planned somewhere in Pennsylvania. Now he kept an eye on the woods so he would not be denied a chance to fight in what was soon to happen.

"Yeah, I see what ya mean, but it don't bother me none that they keeps moving us from one place to 'nother. I just do what I'm told to do, and don't worry about nothin' else excepts trying to stay alive. Too many officers makin' far too many decisions for me to keep track of what they's all thinkin'. I'm trustin' them to do the right thing for us. Got no other choice, I reckon!"

******

In the early morning hours of July 2nd, having had little to eat or drink the previous day, and barely any sleep as well, the 15th Alabama received orders to move out. They had rested for a meager fifteen minutes when the order to move out had been given to them. Despite their fatigue and hunger, they began a roughly twenty-eight mile march to rejoin their division near the Gettysburg battlefield. It would take them only eleven hours to complete this march. This long and tiring march would be one that General Longstreet would later compliment them on making in such a short period of time. The conditions they had marched in had been far less than ideal. By the time they reunited with the rest of their division, Louis passed on hearing about the compliment as his body, like those of his friends, just craved sleep. But there would be little time for sleep on this day as what was about to come their way would long be remembered by the surviving members of the 15th Alabama during each and every one of their remaining days here on earth.

******

On the evening of July 1st, and into the late morning hours of July 2nd, and still operating somewhat blindly due to absence of Stuart's cavalry, an equally tired Robert E. Lee began to formulate his battle plan for the second day of the fight. He did so from his headquarters near the Chambersburg Pike.

In putting his plan together for the day, Lee was forced to rely on information provided to him by two inexperienced scouts. It would later prove to be flawed information that part of the day's battle plan had been based on. With Stuart's cavalry still not present at Gettysburg, Lee was forced to accept the information he was being given by these scouts as being accurate. By using these two scouts, and by not using other more experienced cavalry members who were present, Lee unknowingly sealed his fate for Day Two. The flawed information would contribute to the tragic consequences of the day for the Confederate army.

In the early morning hours of Day Two, Lee sent several scouting parties out; each with different assignments to complete. One of these parties was led by Captain Samuel Johnston, a member of Lee's staff. With him went Major John Clarke, Longstreet's chief engineer, and several others. They were directed to scout the Union's left flank. Lee's somewhat vague and ambiguous orders were for these two officers to simply identify the position of the Union's left flank.

Reporting back to Lee later that morning, Johnston claimed that during their assignment, one that took a few hours to complete, that after leaving the protection of Seminary Ridge, they had crossed over the Emmitsburg Road, and then had scouted the peaks of both Round Top and Little Round Top. In scouting these hills, as well as other adjacent areas, they had found few Union soldiers to be present, most of who were simply passing through the locations they had scouted. Based on this information, and on other information that he had either personally gathered from a morning ride himself, or later learned of, late in the morning Lee soon prepared the finishing touches to his battle plan for the day. The attacks that he would soon outline to his generals would be ones that were doomed to fail. They would fail as it would later become obvious that both officers had not gone to either of the two hills as they said they had, or that their information was incorrect because they had scouted the wrong locations. On Day Two, the Confederate army would move out, in part, on the basis of information that two inexperienced scouts had provided to Lee. Doing so would give historians and Civil

War scholars the additional opportunity to question Lee's decision making skills during the battle of Gettysburg. His decisions would also be affected by other outside factors as well. Those factors would include the lack of sleep, food, and water that many of his men had received over the past few days. Other contributing factors would include the lack of coordination between the various commands that day, and the lack of communication between several Confederate officers during the fighting that occurred that afternoon. The attacks that took place this late afternoon would also be doomed, in part, due to the terrain his army would have to fight over, and due to the presence of late arriving Union troops on Little Round Top.

******

Flushed with success from the actions of his army on the first day of fighting at Gettysburg, Lee devised a plan of attack that would be talked about for generations to come. It was a plan that several of his generals, including Longstreet, and John Bell Hood, disagreed with. Longstreet, in part, disagreed with the frontal assault taking place until all of his divisions had been called up to the front. At this time, General George Pickett's Division had yet to arrive. Despite efforts to talk Lee out of executing the part of his plan that was to attack the Union left, efforts repeatedly made by Longstreet, Lee would not allow changes to be made to the plan. This plan would require the men of the 15th Alabama, along with other regiments from Hood's division, to attack the very left end of the Union line.

It would be a fight that would soon pit the 15th Alabama against a very formidable foe. It would also occur over terrain that was perhaps even more formidable than the terrain that other Confederate regiments encountered that afternoon in Devil's Den. Longstreet's inability to talk Lee out of this portion of his plan, or to at least modify it by allowing Hood's troops to proceed further south around the two small hills, would cost the Confederate army the lives of many of their best soldiers that day.

The task of trying to take a hill the Union army initially referred to as "Rock Hill", or "Sugar Loaf", or "Granite Hill", and one that

Confederate officers simply called "the mountain", would prove to be too big a task for the 15th Alabama, and the other Confederate troops that fought there. Little Round Top would be the scene of one of the bloodiest battles of the war. Many men of the 15th Alabama would finally get to rest there. It was rest that would cause them to never see Alabama again.

II

BAYONETS!

"Hold this Ground at all Hazards!"

COLONEL STRONG VINCENT TO COLONEL JOSHUA CHAMBERLAIN,
JULY 2ND, 1863, AS VINCENT PLACED THE 20TH MAINE
ON THE UNION'S LEFT FLANK AT LITTLE ROUND TOP.

The long march, one that was roughly sixty-seven miles in length, and done in just over three hot and humid days, was one that had been far too like so many others they had completed recently. Like the others, this one had also caused the road's dust to hit the men's sweaty faces and uniforms. The combination caked the men in a layer of wet crusty dust that made the days even more miserable than they already were from the seemingly ever present heat and humidity. After the long and miserable march, the tired and exhausted men of the 20th Maine finally arrived in Gettysburg on the morning after the battle had commenced.

As other regiments were placed in position in and along the battle lines that morning, the 20th Maine was held in reserve behind the Union lines. They were placed in position in a large open field near Rock Creek and Culp's Hill, and told to await further orders. The news that they were not immediately going into battle gave the men a chance to get cleaned up to some degree in the nearby creek, but more importantly it gave them time to rest.

Prior to falling asleep, some of the men, William included, walked forward towards the Union's long line of defense that was located just off of Taneytown Road. From there they could see what they soon would be facing. The loud noises they heard, of both muskets and cannons being fired, some close by, and some off in the distance, told them that the biggest fight of their lives was about to happen. Experienced soldiers by now, they were still shocked by what they saw unfolding, especially the enormity of it. It now looked to them as if the whole Union army had met to fight this one battle at Gettysburg. They quickly saw several different regiments from Pennsylvania, New York, Massachusetts, and Connecticut being marched to their positions along the developing line. As they watched what was happening, they even saw a couple of the other Maine regiments moving towards their position in the line as well. The men could not help but to wave excitedly to their fellow soldiers from back home.

"Tarnation! Looks like we all are here to fight today! Likely the whole dang rebel army is also gonna be here by the looks of it." William had some trouble comprehending the magnitude of what he was seeing in front of him. It was quickly becoming a very impressive sight to see. The others standing with him, Private Gilman Huff, Private Almon Carr, Private Samuel Lowell, and a few others, were also in awe of what was unfolding in front of them.

"Come on, boys! Fall back to our position. We're gonna be in the thick of it soon enough. Need to get some rest so we're ready when we're called. Fall back!" Despite wanting to keep on watching what they were seeing unfold in front of them, the men quickly realized that Sgt. Greenwood was correct. They had to take advantage of whatever brief time they had to rest.

They had spent the better part of the last six days, as well as this very same morning, marching into Pennsylvania, headed for the fight that had started without them. With little to eat during that time, and constantly being on their feet, they welcomed the chance they had to rest. It would soon prove to be a very short period of time.

******

As the men of the 20th Maine rested, Colonel Chamberlain was forced to deal with a somewhat unique problem. Forced to confront a group of soldiers from the 2nd Maine who had threatened 'mutiny' over an enlistment issue, Chamberlain quickly convinced all but a small group of men to join his regiment for the fight that was about to unfold. Skillfully he had quickly bolstered the ranks of his regiment for the fight they were about to enter. The men from the 2nd Maine would soon prove to be a valuable asset to have later that afternoon.

******

As the morning slowly developed, Major General George Meade, who had replaced Hooker on June 28th, began to position his troops along the long Union battle line. It soon would stretch from the area in and around Culp's Hill, and would extend in a long straight line along Cemetery Hill and along Cemetery Ridge, ending just before two small hills. Part of his plan that day was to keep his interior line as short as possible. Doing so would make it easier to resupply the line with new troops, cannons, and other needs as the fighting progressed throughout the day. It would be a part of the plan that later proved to be a well-thought out idea by Meade.

Late in the day, somewhere close to 4 pm, Meade became aware of the intense exchange of cannon fire, and of the fighting that had just begun on the far left flank of the Union line. This fighting had commenced as Lee had begun to send his right flank towards the Union's far left in an attempt to dislodge them from the positions they held in and along Cemetery Ridge. Directing General Gouverneur Warren, the chief engineer of the Army of the Potomac, to investigate what was occurring, while he himself prepared to meet with General Daniel Sickles near the Peach Orchard not far from Devil's Den, Meade would soon learn of the significant problems facing his left flank. One of the problems that both Meade and Warren would quickly learn was that General Daniel Sickles' Third Corps was in the wrong position along the battle line. Unhappy with the position he had been assigned to defend along the Union line, Sickles silently defied Meade's orders and moved his men almost a mile forward of the rest of the line. It would be a tactical move that soldiers, historians, Civil War buffs, and many others, Sickles and Meade included, would criticize, defend, and debate over for years and years. Doing so now left the remainder of the Union left susceptible to attack by Confederate troops. It also made it far more difficult for Meade to be able to support Sickles' exposed position with reinforcements and supplies. In scouting Sickles' new position, Warren quickly realized that Sickles had not only defied Meade's orders regarding what position he was to take along the Union line, but that he had also failed to position a part of his corps on Little Round Top to serve as protection against the Confederacy being able to turn the Union line.

By failing to anchor part of his corps on Little Round Top as Meade had directed him to do, Sickles caused an earlier concern of Warren's to now come true. Earlier in the day, Warren had spoken about a fear of seeing the Union line being turned by the Confederate army. Now seeing that Little Round Top had been left relatively unmanned, he realized that his earlier concerns were now a distinct possibility. The Union's left flank was soon to be tested by Colonel William C. Oates and his 15th Alabama.

While neither Meade nor Warren could have possible known this at the time, one of the orders that was being given to Oates, as he stepped off with his men, was for him to *try and turn the Union line. Inflict as much damage as you can.* Seizing Little Round Top would afford him the opportunity to do just that.

While viewing the problem that Sickles had caused from a position he had taken on top of Little Round Top, Warren had first seen the hill being unoccupied as an issue of immediate concern. The small, but now important hill was being manned by only a handful of Union signalmen. Immediately after sensing that concern, he saw an even bigger problem about to unfold. It was then, while viewing the area out in front of him through his binoculars, that Warren saw the sun reflecting off the bayonets of Confederate troops as they huddled in the woods off to the southwest of Little Round Top. Quickly realizing the Confederate troops could easily threaten the exposed left flank of the Union line from either Round Top or Little Round Top, and that they could move to attack the rear of the Union line from these positions as well, Warren sent his three aides, Captain Chauncey Reese, Lt. Washington Roebling, and Captain Ranald MacKenzie, to seek additional help so troops could be placed on Little Round Top. Warren's actions would quickly thrust the 20th Maine into the heat of battle.

General Warren's observations that day, and his subsequent actions of quickly having Union troops moved to the crest of Little Round Top, caused him to be considered one of the heroes of Little Round Top. His actions that day have caused him to be long remembered by the ages.

******

Soon learning of Warren's concerns from Captain MacKenzie, Colonel Strong Vincent, the commanding officer of the Fifth Corps, 1st Division, 3rd Brigade, quickly brought his one thousand men, including the 20th Maine, up near the crest of Little Round Top. Deploying them in a long line, he assigned the 20th Maine the extreme left position in the entire Union line. To their right, he deployed the 83rd Pennsylvania, the 44th New York, and the 16th Michigan. For now, Round Top would remain unmanned as time did not allow for additional troops to occupy it.

As Vincent expressed the importance of the position the 20th Maine now occupied to Colonel Chamberlain, he told the Maine commander *"this is the extreme left flank of the Union battle line. You must hold this position at all costs!"* Those words reinforced to Chamberlain the importance of the position he now commanded.

Deploying his men into positions close to the crest of the hill, Chamberlain stretched them out as far as possible in a single line so they could support each other as best as possible. To his extreme left, but detached from his main part of the line, he sent out Company B to protect his rear from enemy attack. Those men would later be joined by others from the 2nd U.S. Sharpshooters.

Speaking to his company commanders, as Vincent had done with him, Chamberlain stressed the importance of the position they now occupied. "Men, we cannot fall back. We must hold this position at all costs! We need to be ready for what quickly will be upon us. Tell the men to gather whatever they can, rocks, dirt, tree branches, and have them construct some breastworks to help protect themselves from what is about to happen."

******

As Chamberlain was desperately trying to reinforce his line, General Warren was desperately trying to do the same along the entire left flank of the Union line. With the assistance of Colonel Vincent, and others, he had quickly gotten the men into position. Now it was time to reinforce the line with more firepower.

Seeing the difficulty that some of the gunners were having in getting the six three-inch ten-pound Parrott rifles of Lt. Charles Hazlett's Battery D up the steep slopes of Little Round Top, Warren, assisted by several of Vincent's men, quickly pitched in to help them move the artillery pieces up closer to the crest of the hill.

As the cannons finally reached the crest of the hill, Warren positioned them to the far right of Vincent's men. From there he hoped they could support the line of men that stretched from the positions held on the right by the 16th Michigan all the way to the end of the left flank, the position held by the 20th Maine. Almost immediately the somewhat limited effectiveness of the cannons became known. Hazlett quickly sought out Warren to advise him of the problem that faced his artillerymen.

"General, my men are firing away as fast as they can reload, but only with limited success. We can pound away at the Rebs in and around Devil's Den, and over at Houck's Ridge, but we can't support your line very effectively."

The bad news did not sit well with Warren, and he quickly stopped barking orders to others so he could listen to what else Hazlett had to tell him. The loud noise of two successive cannon rounds being fired caused both Warren and Hazlett to momentarily flinch before they resumed their conversation.

"Lieutenant, the men need the support of your cannons. What's the problem you are facing?"

"General, from where my cannons are situated behind your line we cannot get the correct angle we need to fire down this steep grade. Even if we bring the cannons forward we won't be able to fire down the slope like you want us to. The hill is just too steep for us to make it work! I've tried moving my position a couple of times already to see if I can make it work, but we just cannot get the angle we need to be able to fire down the hill. I've already lost three of my men trying to do just that; had to replace them with a couple of my drivers and with a couple of your soldiers. The Reb snipers down in the area of the Slaughter Pen are creating havoc within the ranks of my men. My boys are also getting worn out from having to carry the powder and the ammunition up the hill from where we had to leave the supply wagons."

Warren was frustrated by the news he heard, but then Hazlett gave him some good news. "General, I don't care what we can hit with these cannons, but we will keep firing away at the Rebs the best we can. We'll keep pouring the rounds into them! We may not be able to support the line in front of you as much as we had hoped we could, but the sounds of my cannons firing will help the morale of the men along the line. I'll keep the guns firing as long as I can!"

After turning to leave, Hazlett passed on the orders to Lt. Benjamin Rittenhouse so he also knew what was expected of them. Shortly after doing so, Hazlett was dead. Shot in the head by a Confederate sniper.

******

Fortunate to fall into a position along the center of the 20th Maine's line, one that afforded him some protection behind two small maple trees, William quickly placed a small pile of rocks and some dead tree branches in front of him to protect him further from the Confederate musket fire that was about to come his way. To his left and right, Harlow Dunbar and Albert Moody did the same. Soon the others from the 20th Maine had also collected enough rocks, dirt, and dead branches that a small stonewall afforded the regiment some protection. As he quickly worked to enhance his own position, William kept one eye down the steep slope in front of him, watching to see if unwanted guests were approaching his position.

"Harlow, ya scared over what's 'bout to come charging our way from up the hill? I know I am!" William wasn't afraid to admit his feelings to his friend as he knew this day could be his last one on earth.

Working as fast as he could to fortify the ground in front of him, Harlow spoke to his friend. "Only a dang fool wouldn't admit he weren't scared today. I can feel my heart beatin' right fast. Yeah, I'm nervous; scared too! Ain't afraid to admit it either. Sure am glad we got the high ground for this here fight. Pity those Johnnies who got to climb up this steep slope. Gonna be tough on them to make it this far, and I'm gonna do my part to see they don't! I'm gonna make this feel like Fredericksburg all over again, 'cepting this time we got the high ground."

Finished with his work, William surveyed the rocky terrain out in front of their position. "Yer right about that, Harlow. Those trees, along with those big boulders, not mentioning how steep this hill is, well . . . well, let's just be glad we're here and they ain't. At least not right now they ain't! I know I wouldn't want us to be the ones trying to take this position. Wonder how many of them are coming after us today?"

Harlow's answer to his friend's question was short and accurate. It would also soon prove to be the correct one. "Too many, I reckon."

******

"Here they come, boys! Here they come!"

In moments, the first Confederate volley was fired at the Union line. Like the one that followed, the first two volleys were fired high over the heads of the soldiers manning the Union line. Both volleys smashed into trees immediately behind the Union line, the bullets stripping bark off the trees in many areas, snapping branches off tree limbs, and causing a cascade of shredded leaves to fall to the ground like snowflakes. Quickly the accuracy of the Confederate soldiers got better, and bullets now tore into Union soldiers instead of tearing into trees and vegetation like they had.

The first warning cry had come off to the right of William's position as the 44th New York had just gotten into their fixed positions. Immediately they were attacked by several regiments belonging to General Evander Law's Alabama Brigade, as well as soldiers from Arkansas and Texas who were assigned to General Jerome Robertson. The 4th Alabama and 48th Alabama, as well as other Alabamians, and the 4th Texas and 5th Texas, quickly began to attack the position held by the New Yorkers. Some of the attackers had come up and over Round Top, made their way through the woods, and then come up the rocky slope of Little Round Top, while others had come directly up the steep slope of the hill. Looking out in front of his position, William and his fellow soldiers watched carefully as more and more Confederate soldiers started to appear, the dense foliage near the base of the hill no longer able to hide them as they advanced up the hill.

Quickly the attackers struck the right side of the Union line again, but like the first time they were repulsed by the men from New York. Beaten back twice, and sustaining a significant number of losses, the two Texas regiments, and the 4th Alabama, moved away from the fight. As other Confederate soldiers regrouped within the protection afforded to them by the woods and large boulders near the base of the hill, they prepared to come at Colonel Vincent's men again. As they did, Colonel William Oates' 15th Alabama, along with the 47th Alabama, were making their way towards the position held by Chamberlain and the 20th Maine.

******

It only took a few minutes for a good part of the Union's left flank to now become engaged in an intense fight with the Alabamians. Quickly the fighting grew more and more intense as the minutes slowly passed by. As the battle raged between the 20th Maine and the 15th Alabama, Chamberlain was forced to adjust his line to meet the new challenges thrown at him by Oates and his men. Forced to adjust his line as the 15th Alabama moved further to his left, Chamberlain took soldiers from other positions within his own line and supported his left with these men. Quickly they successfully beat back brave charges made up the hill by both the 15th Alabama and 47th Alabama, significantly thinning the number of attackers during each charge they made. The Alabamians were not the only ones being punished during this withering fire that was being exchanged between the two sides as the 20th Maine was also taking on casualties within their ranks as well.

Firing, reloading, and firing time after time, William watched as the rebel soldiers began to move closer to the positions of the 44th New York and 83rd Pennsylvania. A veteran of several fights and battles by now, he was still shocked by what he saw coming at him. This was quickly becoming the most intense fight he had been in. Fighting to stay alive, he still could not help but to admire the bravery of the Confederate soldiers as they tried and tried, with little or no protection, to overtake the Union positions they were attacking. Starting to reload his musket again, he saw help coming to support the 44th New York and the 83rd Pennsylvania. He would later find out it had been the 140th New York who had arrived to support their fellow soldiers along the line of battle. As he finished reloading his musket, he shot a quick glance back to his right. Quickly he saw a group of Alabamians melt away from a ferocious volley fired at them by the remaining men of the 44th New York.

"Dang!"

It was all William could think of to say when he saw the effect of the deadly volley of fire the 44th New York had just poured into the advancing soldiers from Alabama. Lying on the ground, where moments ago they had been running to attack the Union line, were the bodies of eight dead Confederate soldiers.

All along the Union line where William and the others fired volley after volley down the hill at their attackers, the sheets of hot lead fired from their muskets had caused flames to spit out from the ends of their barrels each time the powder burned to fire another round. Soon the smoke, some of which had come from Hazlett's cannons, lingered in the air as more and more gunpowder burned with each shot that was fired. The smell of burnt gunpowder, and the sounds of men dying, blanketed the hill in front of the Union line.

Soon beating back another brave attack by the 15th Alabama, the men from the 20th Maine let out a brief cheer. To some, the cheer had been let out because they had beaten back another serious challenge thrown at them, but for William it simply meant he had survived another brush with death. Directly in front of him, one of the branches he had set out to protect his position was pocked with two bullet holes. The dead branch that he had placed in front of his position had already served its purpose. Seeing what the branch had stopped caused him to slowly breathe a sigh of relief. Not ten feet in front of the positions that Harlow and he were occupying were three dead Confederate soldiers. As he stared at the bodies, he figured they had likely been the ones who had fired the rounds that the tree branch had stopped. Despite being hot and sweaty from the heat of the day, William felt a cold chill run down his back as he thought about what might have happened to him if he had not placed the branch in front of him. Closing his eyes very briefly, he thanked the Lord for saving him from sustaining a serious injury or death. "Thank you, Lord! I owe you one for sure!"

William was quickly snapped out of his moment of self-reflection. "I told ya, boy! I told ya, didn't I!" cried Harlow. "This steep hill is like having another hundred men with us. Them Rebs ain't gonna get too far today! No, siree! They ain't gettin' us today!"

Harlow's statement would later prove to be an accurate prediction of how the day would play out. But despite the steep grade, and the withering fire they would have to slowly work their way through, the brave soldiers of the Confederacy would soon get further up the steep hill than many would have thought. Their valiant efforts would soon cost the 20th Maine several more men.

******

Driven back down the hill, the weary soldiers from Alabama quickly reformed. Despite being fatigued from their long overnight march, and exhausted from the heat and lack of water, they now charged back up the hill again yelling like a group of banshees. Again they moved further to their right to attack the line held by Chamberlain's men. Despite being staggered with losses from the deadly fire poured into them, the 15th Alabama continued to attack as they made their way up the hill. Soon they were beaten back once again, but not before inflicting a serious number of deaths and injuries among the men who manned the small set of Union breastworks.

After they had taken time to regroup, they soon came back at the 20th Maine by coming up and over Round Top, using whatever cover they could find to mask their approach. As they moved closer to the Union line, off to William's left he heard Chamberlain holler out another warning. *"Here they come again, boys! Be ready to fire!"* Then, in William's mind, for just a few brief moments, the fighting that unfolded right in front of him seemed to somehow now take place in very slow speed. It was something that had never happened to him before. The momentary lull he experienced was quickly broken by Chamberlain's next loud command.

"Fire!"

Another deadly volley was quickly fired down the hill towards the advancing Alabamians. Despite taking on the deadly fire the 20th Maine had thrown at them, more and more men from the 15th Alabama surged forward towards the depleting Union line. As they did, they exchanged volleys of fire with the men protected by the low stonewall. In moments, one more lethal volley of fire, this one fired by the soldiers occupying the center of the 20th Maine's position, blew a gaping hole in the line of the advancing Alabama soldiers. Quickly, nine Confederate soldiers fell dead; doing so in a small pile just yards before reaching the low stonewall. At nearly the same time, and just yards down the line, several men from the 15th Alabama finally reached the small stonewall they had desperately been trying to reach with each of their charges. Now they briefly engaged members of the 20th Maine in vicious hand-to-hand combat for several minutes before being beaten back. Several men from each side were beaten badly in this intense fighting as muskets were wildly swung as soldiers, with no time to reload their muskets, attempted to defend themselves from being bayoneted or injured in some similar manner. The toll on both sides of the fight was now becoming enormous.

As William continued to fire at the advancing Alabamians, he did whatever he could to avoid being shot as he reloaded his musket each time. Loading his musket while lying on his back at times had taken a couple of more seconds than it would normally have taken, but by doing so he avoided being struck several times by the bullets that whizzed by over the top of the small stonewall.

Reloading his musket once again, William heard a voice call out to him. "Ya doing OK, William?"

The voice came from Sergeant Andrew Tozier, the Color Company flag bearer for the 20th Maine. Standing there as he held the regimental flag, and while helping to somehow load rifles for those around him, Tozier was a sign of inspiration for William. He was quickly struck by the sergeant's bravery as bullets, shards of tree bark, and chips of rock, from bullets striking the rocks that had been piled up around them, flew by him. Amazingly, Tozier did not have a mark on him. Seeing the flag still standing gave William, and several others, the thought that the 20th Maine was still very much alive in this brutal fight.

"Yeah, I'm doing OK! I'm just sorry that they aren't." To his right, William gave a nod of his head, pointing Tozier in the direction of where the bodies of Corporal John Foss and Private Seth Clark lay.

"They died doing their duty," Tozier bluntly replied, "brave lads, both of them!"

William took in Tozier's words for a moment, and then prepared to fire another round at the still advancing Confederate soldiers. "That is one brave man," he thought to himself as he took one last look at the sergeant calmly standing there watching what was happening up and down the line.

******

As the 15th and 47th Alabama regiments pressed on with their attacks, Chamberlain learned that his men were beginning to run low on ammunition. He also saw the threat that another attack might have if the Alabamians regrouped and attacked them again near the position his men were struggling to hold onto. It was Chamberlain's exposed left flank, the very end of the Union line. He now considered it a strong likelihood that the Confederates could possibly turn his left flank if his own men ran out of ammunition. Soon he asked himself a question. "How much longer can we possibly hold our position, and how can I be expected to hold it if we don't have any ammunition to fire?"

Chamberlain was now forced to realign his men, doing so as an uncoordinated attack by twenty soldiers of the 15th and 47th Alabama regiments tried to hit the right side of his line. As these soldiers advanced closer towards the Union line, they were met with a deadly volley of musket fire, and six more Confederate soldiers fell dead. Wisely, the others quickly retreated to safety back down the hill.

Believing he had to reinforce his left flank with men from the right side of his line, but at the expense of leaving the right side weakly defended, Chamberlain was now forced to do so. His now weakened line, once manned by several soldiers in almost every position, was down to a single soldier in each position. The threat now was clearly to his left. After two more even deadlier exchanges of musket fire between the two opposing regiments, the Alabamians retreated for one last charge. The brief respite gave Chamberlain, William, Sgt. Tozier, and the others, a chance to catch their breath, and to collect their thoughts.

Slowly standing up from the kneeling position that he had just fired his musket from, William saw Chamberlain intently watching the Confederate soldiers as they retreated back into the tree line. "We're giving them a good lickin', colonel! Those men who keep coming at us are a brave bunch, but we have the high ground, and they aren't gonna get it from us today!" William's enthusiasm was greeted by a tired smile from Chamberlain as he leaned back against a small tree to wipe the sweat off of his face.

"Keep up the good work, William! I've seen what you and the others have been doing since the fighting commenced. You all are doing well today to keep them away from us. God willing, we will prevail!" Chamberlain's comment caused a few other men, who heard what he had said, to also voice their support of both men's comments.

"They ain't gonna beat us today, colonel, no way!"

"He's right, colonel! We'll stay here all day if that's what it takes."

Despite being inwardly calm, he nervously wondered how to maintain his assigned position. Already planning his next move in his head, and already aware of the fact that his men were low on ammunition, Chamberlain simply smiled at his men's comments. He knew that Vincent had sent men, including Captain John Clark, and Captain Amos Judson, out to find additional soldiers and ammunition for needs along the line, but neither of those two needs had yet to reach his position. The weak smile hid the question he was again posing to himself. "How can I maintain our position if we don't have any ammunition?" He would soon come up with the answer to his own question.

******

Up and down the Union line each of the regiments had taken on casualties. While the stand they had made had already cost the lives of many soldiers, it would soon cost them many more. Among the Union dead already were Colonel Strong Vincent, Brigadier General Stephen Weed, Colonel Patrick O'Rorke, of the 140th New York, and Lt. Charles Hazlett, of the Fifth Corp's Artillery Brigade.

******

Charged at by both the 15th Alabama and 47th Alabama on at least four occasions already, the 20th Maine quickly prepared for at least one more attack with the remaining ammunition they had available.

Acutely aware of his men being low on ammunition, and likely having enough for only one more stand against an aggressive foe, Chamberlain made plans for the 20th Maine to hold their positions one more time. Gathering his company commanders, he issued his orders to them from near the tree he had briefly been resting against. The small tree sat within a few feet of the small stonewall the men had constructed. Barely twelve feet off the ground, the tree's bark had been forcefully broken off after being riddled by Confederate bullets. "Tell the men they need to be accurate when they fire; tell them we need to conserve our ammunition. Have them check the dead and injured for any available ammunition as well."

Realizing more than ever the importance of the position his men held, Chamberlain reinforced it to his company commanders before he sent them back to their positions along the wall. "We must hold this position at all costs! If we don't, our whole left flank will cave in, and the Rebs will be free to threaten our whole line. Rally the men however you chose, but don't fall back. Hold the line!" Pausing for a moment as he surveyed the line around him, and the scene in front of him, Chamberlain stunned his officers with his next order. "Tell the men to fix bayonets!" Then he told his commanders what his plans were for the regiment when the ammunition ran out.

The order was quickly given to fix bayonets, and the order of *'Bayonets!'* resonated up and down the line of the 20th Maine. Quickly the sound of steel bayonets could be heard as they were affixed to the ends of the men's muskets.

William looked at both of his friends as the order to fix bayonets was given. "Fix bayonets? Does that mean we're gonna charge down the hill at them, or does it mean we're gonna wait it out here for them to come at us?" The vagueness of the order confused him, and the thought of stabbing someone with his bayonet in hand-to-hand combat scared him even more than he already was.

"I guess when we see the boys on the left go over the wall we'll know, won't we?" The calmness in Harlow's voice did little to calm William down.

The order to fix bayonets had barely been given when the next cry was heard off to the left of the line.

"Here they come again!"

The chilling call quickly caused Chamberlain, and the men on the left of the line, to see the remaining soldiers of the 15th and 47th Alabama regiments advancing through the woods. Waiting for the Alabamians to get as close as possible, the 20th Maine fired what little ammunition they had left. Then reacting to the next order they heard, the men from Maine sprung over the low stonewall with bayonets fixed to their muskets. Quickly they charged downhill at the now retreating Alabamians.

Sweeping down the hill from left to right, Chamberlain's men fought some of the retreating soldiers from the 15th Alabama in bitter, but brief, incidents of hand-to-hand combat. Killing some, injuring more, and capturing even more of the 15th Alabama, as well as stragglers from other nearby regiments, the unexpected actions of the 20th Maine caused some of the remaining Confederate soldiers to flee to safety in several different directions. Quickly, some of Chamberlain's men charged after the fleeing soldiers until they heard the regiment's bugler sound recall. Stopping their pursuit, they hurried back to fall in with the others near the base of Little Round Top. As some of the Alabamians continued in their efforts to avoid being captured, confusion spread through their ranks. For some retreating soldiers of the 15th Alabama, their long and arduous day ended tragically as they now strayed too close to the hidden position of Captain Walter Morrill, and his men of Company B of the 20th Maine. Standing with them now were members of the 2nd U.S. Sharpshooters. This brief and deadly skirmish between both sides resulted in additional losses for Oates' Alabama regiment.

Despite the slopes of Little Round Top being covered with the dead and wounded, and despite the likelihood that many Confederate soldiers were still in the immediate area, many of Chamberlain's men paused briefly around him after the bugle had sounded recall. After catching their breath from the charge they had made down the hill in pursuit of the retreating rebel soldiers, they let out a loud yell. *"Hooray, Hooray!"* It was more of a yell of relief about being alive than it was a yell of celebration for defeating the enemy. It was a yell they repeated twice more before they started moving their prisoners back up the hill.

******

As the bitter and brutal fighting came to an end on Little Round Top, Chamberlain's men gathered up the few hundred prisoners they had taken, tended to their own injuries, and collected what ammunition they could find from the bodies of the dead that littered the slopes of the hill. For now, the dead and wounded, some of whom fell in small piles, and some who fell still clutching their muskets, were far too many to count. It was a sight that no soldier enjoyed seeing that day.

Watching as his men rounded up their remaining prisoners, Chamberlain walked back up the hill to check on his wounded men. In spots along the line, he briefly paused to offer reassuring words to those soldiers who had been injured. As he finished speaking with Private Andrew Morrill, who had been shot in his upper right arm, Lt. Thomas Chamberlain, serving as his brother's adjutant, called down the line to him. "Colonel, can you come here, please!"

The urgency in Tom's voice was noticeable, and Chamberlain quickly moved to where his brother was kneeling down besides an injured soldier. As he got closer to where his brother knelt on the ground, he could see two other soldiers helping to care for an injured soldier. Soon he saw that it was Private George Washington Buck, of Company K, who had been injured. It was easy to see that Buck had likely sustained a mortal wound to his chest.

Private Buck, formerly a sergeant in the 20th Maine, had been demoted prior to Gettysburg due to an incident with an officer. Now aware that he was dying, Buck sought to have a few last words with his colonel.

Trying to comfort the dying man lying on the ground in front of him, Chamberlain softly spoke first. "George, are you doing OK? I saw you giving it to the Rebs pretty good during the early part of the fight. I'm proud of how ya helped us today!"

"Colonel, thanks for stopping to see me. I know I'm hurt pretty bad, likely a goner, but that's just how it is. I ain't upset over it as I know I did my part to help the boys today. Before I leave ya, I . . . I want ya to know I'm sorry about what happened between me and that officer. I'm sorry if I caused ya any problems." Buck paused a moment to cough, and to spit out a mouthful of blood. As he did, Chamberlain noticed how quickly Buck's shirt had gotten soaked in blood from his chest wound. "I'm proud to have served in this here outfit, colonel, and darn proud to have served with all of these fine men. I also appreciate how ya have treated me, sir. You're a right fine officer!"

Kneeling down next to Buck, Chamberlain sought to comfort him. "George, you're a right fine soldier yourself! All of us have been proud to serve with you as well. Can I do anything for you right now?"

Quiet for a couple of moments as he mustered his remaining strength to answer Chamberlain, Buck's eyes bounced back and forth between the Chamberlain bothers, and to the others around him. Tears soon began to well in his eyes as he knew the end was near for him. "Colonel, if ya would just write a letter to my parents for me, I'd be in your debt. Tell them my last thoughts were of home. Please tell them I said goodbye to each of them before I passed." Exhausted from speaking those few words, and from his loss of blood, Buck fought to catch his breath so he could speak again. "I'm real proud of the fight the boys put up here today! They didn't just fight to stay alive, they fought for our flags, they fought for Maine, and they fought for what this country stands for. Unlike some of them Rebs who dun quit on us, we didn't quit. Please, I beg of you, please tell the boys for me that I was proud to have fought alongside of them today. That's what ya can do for me, if ya will."

Taking Buck's right hand in his, Chamberlain thanked him for his service to the army, and to the regiment. "Sergeant, I'd be honored to write that letter for ya, and I'll be sure to let the boys know your feelings. Consider it done!"

Buck smiled up at Chamberlain for a brief moment. "Ya called me sergeant, sir. I guess you're pretty tired yourself, huh?"

"George, I'm very tired, but I'm still thinking pretty clearly. For all you have done in this dreadful war, and for how you fought so bravely alongside us today, I think you deserve to be a sergeant again. I'll make it official as soon as I can, but from this point on it's officially Sgt. George Washington Buck of the 20th Maine. That OK with you?"

Hearing what Chamberlain had said caused Buck to shed his last few tears, and they slowly ran down his sweat stained face. "I can die a happy man now, colonel. I appreciate your kindness, God bless ya!" Raising his right hand, he gave Chamberlain a weak salute. In moments he was dead.

Standing up, Chamberlain stood stiffly for a few minutes as he looked down on Sgt. Buck. Raising his right hand, he saluted the body of his dead sergeant. Finished with his salute, he spoke his final words to Buck. "Rest in peace, George, rest in peace."

Turning to walk back to check on his other injured soldiers, Chamberlain saw the bodies of First Sergeant George Noyes and Private James Merrill, both of Company K. They had died early in the battle, just like Sgt. Charles Steele of Company A, when the 47th Alabama had first charged their position along the Union line.

******

Early that evening the men of the 20th Maine would have their line extended to the top of nearby Round Top. Confederate sniper fire from down in Devil's Den would harass them for several hours, but for most of the evening, and throughout the rest of the night, it was quiet for Chamberlain's survivors.

Finally able to sit down near the crest of Round Top, at a position about as far away as anyone could be from where the right flank of the regiment's first position had been on Little Round Top, William tended to his two injuries. He had received a slash on his left arm from a Confederate officer's saber when the officer had tried to fight with him and other soldiers near the base of the hill as he was being taken prisoner. He had also sustained a small graze on his left calf from an errant shot fired by a retreating Confederate soldier. Fortunately neither injury was significant. Tending to his calf injury, he took pride in the fact that he had helped to capture the Confederate officer who had slashed him. For a brief moment, as they struggled to subdue the officer they had captured, he had thought about running his bayonet through the officer's chest, but after knocking him to the ground he had quickly seen that whatever amount of fight the officer had left in him that it had quickly dissipated. His revenge for being slashed had been a punch to the officer's face, one that may have broken the Alabamians nose, but he had refrained from senselessly killing the captured officer. As he tended to his wounds, he looked down at the officer's saber, one he now claimed as his. To no one in particular, he proudly boasted out loud, "I'm taking this saber home! It's gonna remind me every day of what I survived on this horrible day!"

Soon finished tending to his injuries, William walked across the crest of Round Top and looked over in the direction of the slopes of Little Round Top. Looking over in the remaining light of the day, he saw what was left scattered across the steep slopes. The sight of the many dead bodies, some in blue, and some wearing grey, was horrible to see. Even worse, the painful sobs of the injured crying out for help was difficult to have to listen to. They were sounds he could not block out. Unable to offer any help to those who lie there injured, their painful cries for help would haunt him at times for the rest of his life.

✶✶✶✶✶✶

"What now, colonel? What are your orders?"

Chamberlain looked over at his brother, Thomas, seated next to him on Round Top. Both of the men had only been resting for a few minutes since tending to their injured men when his brother posed the question to him.

"After we rest here for a few minutes, I want to make sure we have seen to the needs of the men. We need to make sure the wounded are being properly cared for, and are off to a nearby field hospital as soon as possible. I doubt that any more fighting is headed this way today. It's getting dark and everyone's tired after a long hot day, but I want the men to be ready if trouble does come our way. I'll send out a few runners soon to get us some food and water. Make sure you get the men some more ammunition. Some of them still don't have any. Until we receive further orders, I want to maintain our line here as best as possible. Keep some of the men awake so we have lookouts watching up and down the two hills; have some of the men watching our rear as well. I doubt anyone's coming, but let's make sure we're ready just in case they do. I don't want any surprises tonight; the men are too tired for any surprises. Understand?"

"I do, Lawrence, I do."

Chamberlain smiled at his brother, glad that they both had lived through this terrible fight.

******

An extremely tired and slightly wounded, but very happy, William Barton spent the night on the far left of the 20th Maine's newly extended line. He would spend the entire night near the top of Round Top, and would do so reliving what had taken place during the day of bitter fighting. Unlike so many others, he had survived the vicious fighting that had taken place at Little Round Top. Lying on the ground before falling asleep, he dreamed of home, and of a less dangerous life. He also thanked God for being able to have that dream on this moonlit night. For many others, their dreams had died with them earlier in the day.

12

THE 15TH ALABAMA ATTACKS LITTLE ROUND TOP.

"My dead and wounded were then nearly as great in number as those still on duty . . . . The blood stood in puddles . . . . the ground was soaked with the blood of as brave men as ever fell on the red field of battle."

COLONEL WILLIAM C. OATES, C.S.A., ON THE FIGHTING DONE BY HIS 15TH ALABAMA AT LITTLE ROUND TOP.

The battle plan that Lee drew up for July 2ⁿᵈ was one that required General James Longstreet's First Corps to assume a position on the far right of the Confederate line. The plan was one that Longstreet strenuously argued against executing. As he argued against executing a plan that he did not believe in, he also presented the commanding general with an alternative plan to consider. It was one that did not include having to make the frontal assault against the left flank of the Union line that Lee had devised. Others, like General John Bell Hood, also would later take exception to executing the plan, and only carried it out after being ordered to do so by Longstreet. The options now presented to Lee were ones he refused to consider.

Late in the morning of July 2ⁿᵈ, as Lee again discussed his plan with him, and with his other commanders, Longstreet again tried unsuccessfully to have the plan's route of attack on their right flank modified. While not having the chance to inspect the terrain his men would have to fight on, Longstreet still knew from the information he had been provided with that it would be a next to impossible task for his soldiers to accomplish. They had marched all day the day before, and had marched almost the entire night to get to Gettysburg, and now they were being asked to stay awake all day and fight a battle over difficult terrain. Several times he asked for permission to send a brigade of men further south so they could attack the Union line from the rear, but each time Lee refused to risk losing a brigade trying to do so.

As he discussed his concerns with Lee, Longstreet began to develop a similar concern over Lee's health. In the past, Lee had always welcomed alternative options to the plans he had crafted, and had generally allowed his generals to carry out his plans as they saw fit, but now he wanted to hear nothing being said against the plans he had developed. To Longstreet, Lee seemed to have become weak, almost as if he was distracted and confused at times.

Listening to Lee speak, Longstreet's focus continued to be on his general's health. "Is he having another attack of heart problems like he's had in the past, or is it a problem like so many others are having from eating all of those darn cherries that are growing all over the place? Why can't he concentrate like he normally can?" Watching closely for several more minutes, he became convinced that Lee was suffering from a serious case of diarrhea. "Darn cherries!" He quickly thought.

Like a protective father, Longstreet had tried to prevent what he saw as a wasteful slaughter of his men. His position, although supported by Hood, who the commanding general regarded very highly, was not given strong consideration by Lee.

******

Early in the afternoon of Day Two, after a long and slow march to their far right flank, a march that was confusing and made twice over the same dusty roads as they tried to mask their presence from Union observers on Little Round Top, Longstreet and Hood finally arrived close to the area near Little Round Top, and Devil's Den. As confusing as the march was to Longstreet, and to his commanders, due to the route not having been travelled by any experienced scouts as of yet, the hot dusty march was even more confusing to the men.

"Eddie, I don't know about you and the other boys, but I'm bone tired from these past two days of marching. That little break we had last night didn't mean a thing to me as I think I dun woke up even more tired than I were when I went to sleep. Now these generals got us marching back and forth on the same dang road. What is they trying to do? Is they tryin' to find the place that many of us are likely gonna die on today?"

"I ain't sure, Louis, but I'm even more tired than I think I is. I needs some water, some food, a few days of sleeping, and no Blue Bellies looking for a fight, that's what I need!"

Louis smiled a tired smile at his cousin. "It's almost like General Longstreet don't look too happy about what we's up to doing. I heard him barking at some officers earlier that this fight we're about to commence weren't his idea. Heard somethin' being talked about that mentioned moving further south than we's going, but I'm guessing we ain't goin' that way by the looks of Old Pete. He had a mean look in his eye when I seen him earlier. He's fit to be tied, that's fer sure!"

******

Sitting on their horses before going their separate ways later that afternoon, Hood stared at his old friend for several minutes before speaking. He had played out in his head the words he wanted to say, but chose them carefully as he did not want to offend his friend. Summoning up the right words, he spoke by addressing his friend by his nickname.

"Pete, I know you have tried to speak to the old man about this, but I want you to know I'm against this here fight taking place on such terrible ground. The terrain is terrible, the rocks are too big, and far too many to get safely around, and the Union soldiers are sittin' right where they want to be sittin'. Heck, I can almost hear them beggin' us to come get them! Can't blame them as I'd likely be doin' the same if I held the ground they are holding onto." Frustrated at having to execute an order that he clearly saw the danger in, Hood sat quietly on his horse for a few moments before finishing what he had to say. "General, I'm protesting having to execute this here order to you! Can't you talk some sense into the old man? I don't see why he won't come and look over this ground himself. Tell him you and I have a better plan, one that lets the boys get around the backside of these two darn hills. We can hit them hard from the rear, and do so without sacrificing as many of our boys, don't ya agree? This frontal attack is a waste of time, more importantly it's a waste of our men. I can accomplish the same result if you let me go around Round Top, and hit them on their flank and from the rear. The way I want to attack will be far easier on the men! My scouts have told me that we can get to where I want to be by marching through a large field. By doing so, we can also seize a large number of Union wagons my boys have seen; ones that are lightly guarded by only a few men. Lord knows, we need all of the supplies we can find."

Holding his hat in his right hand, Longstreet bowed his head for a brief moment. He knew his friend was right, but he also knew he had tried his best to change Lee's mind several times already. Finally looking up, he hoped his friend could sense the frustration in his voice as he spoke. "General Lee's orders are to attack up the Emmitsburg Road!" Sitting there quietly for several more moments after he finished speaking, he continued to listen to Hood's valid arguments against executing the frontal assault that Lee had already ordered to take place. Despite Hood telling him that his own scouts had told him about a far safer approach to take that afternoon, Longstreet knew Lee still would not listen to any proposed changes to the original plan. He also knew the information that Hood's experienced scouts had given him was likely far more accurate than what the two inexperienced scouts had given to Lee earlier. Now frustrated even more over having to order Lee's plan to be executed so late in the afternoon, and knowing he was out of other options, he tried to calm his tone before he again spoke. "We must obey the orders of General Lee." With that, Hood reluctantly moved out to prepare his men to march towards the waiting Union army.

As Hood rode off to get his troops ready, Longstreet ran an obvious thought through his mind about Lee's plan. "If Hood and I can both see the obvious failure in the proposed plan, why can't he?" It was a thought he would have no real answer to.

******

Despite Hood's strenuous objections, and despite his several attempts to send some of his officers to also try and convince Longstreet not to execute Lee's plan as it was designed, Lee's orders to attack the area in and around Devil's Den, and, unknowingly at this time, Little Round Top, were soon put into motion.

It was late in the day by the time the Confederate attack began, and the lateness of the day would soon spell doom for many. In planning his attack, Lee hoped it would enable his army to seize the area along his right flank. He had given the rocky hill known as Little Round Top little thought during his planning. By seizing the area in and around Devil's Den, Lee hoped it would enable his troops to assault the exposed left flank of the Union army. Among the first soldiers to step forward that afternoon to help execute Lee's plan were the 15th and 47th Alabama regiments. Along with several other Confederate regiments, they soon would become involved in some of the most intense fighting that the war would see.

Soon forced to alter their intended routes of attack due to Union troops moving into the area, and due to the rain of fire being poured down upon them, the 15th Alabama took a more circuitous route to the right than they had been ordered to do. Moving towards the crest of Little Round Top, after advancing on it from Round Top, they attempted to do so by masking their positions as they moved up the steep rocky slopes of the small hill that was now their target. It would be a difficult task to complete for the 15th Alabama as the men were now extremely fatigued. For those men who still had their canteens with them, they had little water to drink during this hot and humid climb.

Partway up the small hill, Louis and Eddie stopped to briefly catch their breath, and to share the last few drops of water in Louis' canteen. Just as they were doing, so soon did others within their company. As they finished off the small amount of water in the wooden canteen, they both again tried to make sense out of what was happening.

"It's far too nice a day to be doin' all this here marching back and forth like we dun before, and now wasting time climbing up and down these two steep hills to go find Yankees to fight. I say let's just tell them boys that today's a day of rest! They don't shoot at us, and we don't bother them. I'm not sure a dang Billy Goat could climb these rocky hills!"

Despite being as tired and thirsty as he was, Louis laughed at Eddie's comment as he stood up to move forward with the others. "Come on ya old Billy Goat, we ain't lettin' the others down. They need us just as we need them. Get yourself up and moving!" Grabbing his tired cousin's right hand, he helped Eddie stand up from the resting position he had been in.

Catching up with the others, Louis and Eddie moved steadily forward up the steep rocky slope. As they moved, with their muskets pointed uphill in the ready position, they took advantage of the heavy growth of shrubs and trees, and the presence of several large boulders. They used the trees and boulders as cover as no one really knew where the Union soldiers had taken up their positions. Not till they were halfway up the hill could they hear the noises that came from near the top of it.

Not sure of what to make from the noises he was hearing, Louis sought to find an answer to the noises from his cousin, and from another nearby soldier that he simply knew by his first name. "Eddie, James! Y'all hear that racket them Blue Bellies are making up there? What'd think they is doing?"

Pausing a brief moment to listen, Eddie quickly figured it out. "Sounds like they are doing what I'd be doing if I were them. Probably fixin' something up there to hide behind so's to make it harder for us to shoot them."

They climbed another sixty feet when the first loud Rebel yell came from off to their left. The left side of the line had moved off before they had, and now those soldiers there were making the first charge at the Union line. Quickly the same yell was repeated several times down the entire line. In moments, Louis saw the entire line begin to rush forward like a giant wave. Briefly watching as the wave of men moved forward, his first thought was that the charge seemed to be done in an uncoordinated manner, almost as if it had been done on an impulse, and one not ordered by any officers. "Why did I not hear any orders being given?" Quickly he was caught up in the charge. As he and other men now rushed forward, the sounds of hundreds of muskets firing at one time could be heard. The noise was deafening. The muskets firing, as well as the firing of several cannons from behind the Union line, caused the air to be filled with smoke and with the acrid smell of gunpowder burning. To Louis' left, where the firing seemed more intense, the screams of men crying out from being shot could soon be heard.

Standing behind a medium sized tree as he reloaded his musket, Louis quickly scanned the Union line before selecting his next target. Through the dense smoke that was hanging over the valley, he saw, both to his left and off to his right, several of his fellow soldiers standing and kneeling in various positions as they reloaded their muskets just like he was doing. Just off to his left, he saw that Eddie was exposed to Union musket fire as he was kneeling down to reload his musket. Concerned for his safety, he quickly yelled to his cousin over the din of the battle. "Eddie, get yourself behind some trees when you're reloading! Don't just kneel out there in the open like a dang fool!" Turning back to face his cousin, Eddie simply nodded his head as he finished his reloading.

Up in front of him, Louis saw the heads of several Union soldiers as they carefully exposed themselves above a small stonewall, selectively firing their muskets down the hill in his direction. Staring at the Union position, he saw heads popping up, muskets then firing, and then the heads disappearing. New heads would then pop up in other places along the Union line. What he saw caused him to ponder the situation he was in. "How in the heck are we ever gonna get to the top of this hill. There's far too many of them shootin' at us from behind a good defensive position for us to get that far! Dagnabbit!" Another quick look up the hill, as he was raising his musket to fire, caused him to see the Union colors waving behind their line. Except for those officers trying to rally their men, the soldier holding the colors was the only person he saw standing up and fully exposed along the Union line. Quickly firing his next shot, Louis' shot missed its mark, and it harmlessly ricocheted off a large tree that a Yankee soldier stood behind. "Dang it all!"

Eddie had now moved to a better position behind a medium sized boulder. Near the very front of the slowly advancing line, compared to where many others from the 15th Alabama now were, he had fired two more shots in the direction of the Union line, hitting one soldier in the left arm. As Louis had done, now he looked up and down his own line to see the progress that others were making as he reloaded his musket once again. As he did, a shot fired at him chipped off a small chunk of the boulder he was hiding behind, and stone dust momentarily got into his right eye. "Dang those Yankee varmits!" It was an obvious thought to have as he annoyingly wiped the dust and sweat from his eye with his right sleeve. Looking to his left, he then saw a sight that caused him to smile and almost cry at the same moment.

Watching him as he ran up the steep hill, Eddie then heard Private John Jordan yelling to his fellow soldiers as he carried the colors of the 15th Alabama towards the stonewall that protected the Union soldiers. *"Follow me, boys!"* Pausing for a moment as he raised his musket to fire, he then saw Jordan slowly fall backwards, dead from a shot through the head. As he fell, Eddie then saw Private William Trimner drop his rifle to the ground, and then seemingly catch the flag before it had even a moment to fall backwards. In moments, Trimner also fell dead, shot through the heart. This time the flag fell to the ground.

As the flag hit the ground, Eddie heard calls for the 15th Alabama to fall back down the hill. What he heard next caused him to do something he never thought he would do. As the bugle had sounded recall, a Yankee cheer had gone up at the same time. The Yankees had seen the Alabama flag fall to the ground. What he heard next motivated him to act quickly.

"I'm gettin' that flag as soon as them Rebs are down the hill!" The brash statement had been uttered loudly by a Union soldier from up behind the small stonewall.

Pausing a brief moment to decide what to do, Eddie sprinted nearly fifty feet across the slope of the hill and picked up the fallen flag. Bullets whizzed all around him as he reached down to pick up the prized souvenir that others wanted so badly. Starting back down the hill, he hollered back over his left shoulder, taunting the Yankees over what he had done. "This here's my flag, Yankee boys! Y'all ain't gettin' it now or never!" A bullet fired from the Union line smashed directly into a tree in front of him as he moved further down the hill. Harmlessly it sent tree bark flying in all directions. "I got the flag, fellas!" Eddie's heroics caused the other members of the 15th Alabama to let out a huge cheer for him. Louis proudly watched as his cousin was warmly greeted by the others as they regrouped near the base of the hill.

Catching his breath at the bottom of the hill, Louis tried unsuccessfully to find some water. By now, everyone's canteens were bone dry. Moving off into the shade, he knelt down to catch a few moments of rest. The feelings of fatigue and thirst he felt were enormous. As he rested, the sights he saw as he had moved back down the hill flashed back through his brain. The steep rocky slope, heavily treed in some areas near the base of the hill, and near barren at the top, had been covered in several locations with the mangled bodies of soldiers from the 15th and 47th regiments. Some were men he knew well, and others were faces that he had recognized, but barely knew. Others he had passed by, injured seriously from being shot by either musket or cannon fire, had cried out for help. Some called for their mothers, while some called for the Lord's help. Many had simply called out for just a drink of water. Resting at the base of the hill, the calls of the injured could still be heard. As it did for him, it also pained the others who briefly were resting around him as they were not able to help their injured friends. The risk of being shot, and not being able to finish the fight they had started, was just too great a risk to take for now.

******

Gathering his men at the base of Round Top, as well as some men from the 47th Alabama, and a few others that had gotten separated from their regiments, Colonel William C. Oates, the commanding officer of the 15th Alabama, told them what he wanted to do next. "The Yankee line seems to be the strongest on our left. We're gonna go up this bigger hill right here, and then we're gonna try and surprise them by coming at them from the far side of this smaller hill. I want us to hit them further to the right of where we did the first time. Y'all use the trees and them large boulders to hide behind so we can get as close as possible to them before they see us. Don't do no talking as your moving along. We need to surprise them as much as we can. Rest here for another couple of minutes while I see how things are going on our left." Pausing to look back at his men after only taking a few steps, he saw their sweating and tired faces looking back at him. "Men, y'all done good in that last charge. I'm rightly proud of ya. We're gonna take it to them Blue Bellies even harder on the next charge we make at them!" His comment caused most of the tired and sweaty faces to smile back at him.

******

Moving closer to the positions occupied by the Union soldiers at the crest of the hill, the Alabamians had no idea of who they were fighting against, nor did they care. They just knew it was Yankees, fighting men just like they were, who held the ground that their Confederate generals wanted them to take for some reason. Despite their increasing fatigue and thirst, the 15th Alabama continued to move up the hill as quietly as possible. The quiet was broken by a call from up near the Union lines. *"Here they come, boys!"* Realizing they had been seen, the Alabama soldiers surged forward as a withering round of fire poured down the hill towards them. Immediately several men fell dead, their fatigue and thirst relieved by a Yankee bullet. A few others had been seriously wounded, and were now unable to fight any longer. Painfully they began to limp and crawl back down the hill to safety.

Despite the intense fire they were taking on, the 15th Alabama held their ground, many even advancing perilously close to the Union line. As fast as possible they raked the Union line with their own deadly accuracy, watching as several Yankees fell either dead or injured. The men from Alabama were not about to leave the field this day without inflicting their own serious damage upon the Union line.

After several more rounds of shots being fired at the protected Yankee positions, Oates sounded a recall to regroup his men and to give them time to briefly rest. It pained him to do so as he knew they had come so close in this charge to making it to the wall. While he had seen a couple of his men make it over the wall, others could not follow them due to the relentless fire they were taking on from up the hill. Despite being frustrated over having to sound the recall, he knew it had been the right thing to do. "I had to sound recall. The men need to rest and we need to reorganize." Watching as his men broke off their attack, and began to withdraw down the hill, another thought entered his mind. "I can only hope that Bobby Lee is as proud of these men as I am!"

******

The next charge up the hill would move the men to the right of the Union line even more. Despite the change in their route to get them to where they wanted to be, and despite the tenacity of how the 15th Alabama fought, Oates' men could not break through in strength to overtake the Yankee position. Several men had died in hand-to-hand fighting after climbing over the wall, and several had crawled back to relative safety after making it to the wall and sustaining significant injuries, but still his men could not breach the wall in sufficient strength. Oates was again forced to sound a recall as his line was being decimated by accurate Union fire. They had gotten so close to the wall this time that several of the men had been shot by Union officers who had helped to defend their line with their pistols. Despite their own losses, they again crippled the line of Union soldiers behind the low stonewall by inflicting additional losses on them as well.

As the Alabama men made their way down the hill once again, several of them paused by the bodies of their dead friends to collect whatever ammunition they could find. They also checked the canteens they found, desperately hoping to find some water to quench their parched throats. They found some ammunition to use during their next charge, but found no water.

******

They had barely gotten to the bottom of the small hill to regroup, when Eddie, despite being as tired and as thirsty as he had ever been, excitedly spoke to his cousin. He was now bleeding from a small laceration near his left eye. "Louis, we nearly got them that time! Dadgummit, we was close! I got to the wall, even shot one of them Yankees in the belly, but then I got whacked on the side of the head by some Yankee's musket. Hurt real bad for a moment, I got to tell ya! I swung my musket at some officer up there, but he blocked it pretty good. Heard him groan a bit, but he still stood there fightin'. Tough son of a gun he must be! Even tried to run his saber through me after I had hit him! Glad to hear the recall sound, I need my belly to eat with. I was glad to be able to skedaddle out of there with all of my parts! Even heard a few bullets whizzing by my head as I was runnin' back down here to meet back up with y'all! I'm right glad to be standing here with ya, I must say!" Finished talking, Eddie dropped to his knees to catch his breath, and to cool down.

Just as fatigued, just as hot, but perhaps even thirstier than his cousin, Louis was still able to manage a smile as he pictured Eddie fighting by the wall, and then running down the hill as he checked to make sure he had all of his parts with him. Kneeling down next to his cousin, he checked to see how bad Eddie's injury was. Despite the amount of blood, he saw it was a rather minor injury. "I'm glad to see ya, Eddie, right glad. But I'd be even more glad to see a canteen of cold water coming my way. I'm so dang thirsty that I think if one of them Yankees gave me even a swig of water that I'd likely throw my musket down right here and never fight against them boys again!"

"We's all likely feeling the same way, Louis. Guess we jus' got to forget about how much we is hurtin' right now. We needs to keep on pushin' up that hill. I know I ain't giving up unless they kills me or captures me. Them Yankees got me all riled up!"

Filling his cartridge box with a few rounds of ammunition he had taken off the dead, Louis looked up the hill to make sure they were not about to be attacked before answering his cousin. "Being hot is bad enough, but I'm dang thirsty. My brain is calling out to me to gets some water; so's my parched throat!" Pausing to breathe deep a few times so he could catch his breath, he then told Eddie what he had experienced during their last attack on the Union positions. "I think I got me at least one last time! I seen a Yankee I fired at go down grabbing the side of his face." He wasn't bragging or gloating over shooting a Union soldier, but for some reason Louis felt the need to tell his cousin what he had done during their last charge up the hill.

After wiping the sweat from his face, Louis spoke again. "When we was coming down the hill I tried to help a couple of the boys as I seen them lying there hurt and all. James Shepherd was one of them.

Ya know who I mean, right? He's that tall skinny boy from over in Pike County, that real tall fella. He was shot bad in the side of his face, right by his right ear. He was a bleeding bad when I seen him. Hope he made it down here OK!"

Too tired to speak, Eddie simply nodded his head a couple of times over what Louis had told him. As it was for so many others, the lack of sleep, but especially the lack of water was now taking a toll on him.

The two men had only rested for a few minutes when Oates gave his next order. Over to his left, he had scouted the progress that other regiments were making against the Union line, but in doing so had learned that several of his fellow officers, including Lieutenant Colonel Benjamin Carter, of the 4th Texas regiment, had either been killed or injured. He had also learned that the 48th Alabama, and the 44th Alabama, had nearly broken through the Union line. Quickly thinking that the intense fighting off to his left would cause the Union to reinforce their threatened position with soldiers that his men had been fighting against, he hoped his men could now make a break in the Union's left flank. Now he prepared his men to move forward as quickly as they could get going. "We're gonna hit them as far to our right as we can. If we can hit that position hard we can start sweeping down their interior lines, and cause them to crumble right before our eyes. Come on, men!" With a renewed conviction, Oates' men moved forward, and so did he. It was against his principles to order his soldiers to fight, and to not be out there leading them forward. Like his men, Oates slowly moved out, silently wondering if he would survive the next charge or not.

As they moved up the slope of the hill, Oates looked back and saw the fatigue in the faces of his tired men. He knew he had to get them moving so they would be ready to fight. Pulling out his pistol, he waved it in the air for his men to see. *"Forward men, to the ledge!"*

Hoping to put an end to this attack, Oates desperately tried to find the extreme left of the Union line as he cautiously advanced up the hill. "If I can get my boys as far to the end of the Union line as possible, we might . . . . we just might be able to turn their line!" Pausing to collect his thoughts, and to give his men time to catch up with him, he drew his saber from his scabbard. With his pistol now in his left hand, and his saber in his right, he again tried to rally his tired group of men. Raising his saber high in the air, he yelled, *"Forward, men, to the wall!"*

Hearing the command, Oates' soldiers rushed forward, but they were only able to move forward another twenty yards or so before they were again greeted with a deadly round of fire being poured into their line. With little cover to hide behind, they bravely stood their ground and exchanged musket and pistol shots with the 20th Maine for several minutes before they heard the next order being given. This time it did not come from Oates.

As the 15th Alabama reloaded their muskets for the last time that day on the rocky slope of Little Round Top, they now saw that instead of the Union line having been thinned out as Oates had hoped, it looked as if it had been reinforced. It was obvious that the Union soldiers had anticipated what the men from Alabama had planned next. Quite smartly, they had reinforced the left side of their line. To Louis and Eddie's dismay; and to Oates as well, the Yankees had guessed right, and they were now waiting for them to attack. The two cousins exchanged concerned looks with each other as they moved cautiously up the steep slope a few more feet. As they moved forward, the next order they and the other members of the 15th Alabama heard was one being cried out all along the Union line. It caused Louis and his friends to cringe when they heard the order being given.

"Bayonets!"

After watching a last brief exchange of fire between both sides, and then realizing that more of his men had again fallen to the accurate and deadly fire laid on them by the Union soldiers, Oates knew that he did not have enough men left to overtake the position occupied by the Yankees. With little recourse, except to hope that his men would live to fight another day, he loudly yelled out his next order. *"To the rear, men! To the rear!"* He had barely given the order when the Yankees bounded over the wall, and started downhill at them with bayonets fixed.

As Oates' men began to retreat, some of them paused to fire back at the Union soldiers who were now charging down the hill after them. Others, simply too tired to run even downhill, gave up and surrendered, begging their capturers for a sip of water. Several other men ran down the hill and followed their flag bearer deep into the tree line, hoping for a safe spot to rest and hide.

While others ran down the slopes of Little Round Top in their efforts to avoid being captured, Oates, followed by some of his other men, ran back up the steep slope of Round Top as they tried to escape. Half-way up the larger hill, he paused to make sure his men were moving out as fast as possible. As he watched them run back towards the Confederate line, he saw one last gory moment take place. Watching as a Yankee soldier tried to tear an Alabama flag from the hands of one of his wounded soldiers, he saw Sgt. Patrick O'Connor, 15th Alabama – Company K, drive his bayonet through the side of the Union soldier's head. Defeated, but still too proud to let his flag be taken from the field as a Yankee souvenir, O'Connor picked up the flag and retreated down the hill. That moment again caused him to realize why he had the pride he had in his men. Satisfied he had done all that he could, he started again up the slope of Round Top, scrambling to get back to safety.

Compared to the war itself, the fighting on Little Round Top had been brief. Like it had been for so many others, the day's heat and humidity, the lack of rest and water, and the stress of fighting a brutal fight against a formidable foe, had also taken a toll on Oates. As he reached the crest of Round Top, his tired legs again caused him to pause and briefly rest. Doing so, he again questioned his own actions during the fighting. "Have I done what my boys expected of me? Did I do what Alabama wanted me to do here today?" Then he pondered one last thought before heading back down the far slope of Round Top. He did so because many of his brave Alabamians, like his own brother, John, and others, like Lt. Barnett Cody and Captain Henry Brainard, had died fighting their last battle there. "Could we have turned their left flank if I just had one more company of men with me?"

As he rested, Oates knew that quite possibly he earlier had that very company of men he needed at his disposal. He now shook his head in disgust over what might have been possible as he knew that company of men had not been used properly in the confusion of the day. It was a group of his men who had been ordered to go with soldiers from other regiments to complete a simple task. It had proved to be anything but a simple task, and it had robbed him of men he needed to storm the

Union position. Earlier that morning, as the commanders of the Army of Northern Virginia wasted valuable time trying to coordinate poorly managed intelligence gathering missions, and as far too much time was wasted while a battle plan was developed for the day, and then argued over, a group of his soldiers had slipped off to complete a task. Time had also been wasted by these commanders failing to properly communicate to the subordinate commanders the actual roles that each division and regiment would have for the day. While the soldiers had left to fill a large number of canteens that belonged to their fellow soldiers, and did so before any regiments had moved out to fight, they never reunited with the regiment.

Oates then questioned a move he had made in the early moments of the fight. As the 15th Alabama had made their way up the saddle area between Round Top and Little Round Top, he sent Captain Francis Shaff's Company A to pursue Union snipers who had been harassing the regiment as they moved forward. Later, he sent the same company to seize several Union wagons that they had observed behind the two hills. Doing so caused Shaff's men to become detached from the regiment for the rest of the day.

As Oates questioned himself on what might have been, it became apparent that the loss of these two groups of soldiers played a role in his regiment not being able to take Little Round Top. "The men did their best for me, and I did my best for them. We all fought hard here today. I will not dwell on what might have been!"

******

Running down the hill as he retreated, Eddie tripped over the roots of a large tree. Losing his balance, he was sent headfirst down the hill for several feet before coming to rest against a large boulder. The speed that he had been running at, coupled with his hard fall, stunned him for a moment after he came to rest against the boulder. Stunned by the fall, plus fatigued past the point of exhaustion, he tried to stand, but fell back down on one knee. As he tried to catch his breath, he cast his now useless rifle off to the side. In his fall, the wooden stock had broken. He was also now out of ammunition. He then slowly tried to stand up again so he could continue further downhill. As he did, other retreating soldiers rushed by him, but no one stopped to help him as they feared doing so would possibly lead them to be taken prisoner by the advancing Union soldiers. Exhausted and dehydrated, he again fell, this time all the way to the ground. Pushing himself up, he hollered out for help. "Louis Hiram Pierce! Where are ya, boy? I need some help! Is ya OK?" Louis Pierce did not answer his cousin's cry for help.

In moments, two Union soldiers roughly grabbed Eddie as he was down on the ground. Soon realizing that he was exhausted and out of the fight, they let go of him and let him rest for a couple of moments. Seeing how bad of shape he was in, one of the soldiers gave him a couple of mouthfuls of water from his canteen. "Have a gulp or two, Reb. Don't drink it all mind you, but have a couple of gulps to quench your thirst somewhat."

After gulping two large mouthfuls of water from the canteen, Eddie soon gave it back to its owner. "Thank you, sir! Thank you! I am plum parched, that helped a bit to calm my throat. I'm parched beyond what a man should be. Hungry too! Thank you for sharing your water with me. I'm much obliged to ya."

Sgt. Timothy Baughman, a tough and gritty senior member of the 20th Maine, and a veteran of many of the war's most significant battles, looked down at the exhausted soldier from Alabama that he had helped capture. He could tell from Eddie's looks that he was now a beaten man. With little regard for the feelings of the soldier who was now lying by his feet, he asked him several questions. "Johnny Reb, ya look a little tired lying there. Ya may not like this question, Reb, but what the heck were you boys thinking trying to take this hill today? You should have known it was too steep to climb, yet alone fight on. Besides being too dang hot a day to fight, we held the high ground; plus you boys didn't bring enough men with you to beat us. Who made the stupid decision to come after us like ya did?"

Still down on all fours, with his head hanging low due to being exhausted, and from being captured, Eddie barely had the strength to look up at the soldier who had been doing all the talking. "General Lee himself made that decision, I guess. Same man who whupped your generals at Fredericksburg and Chancellorsville, that's who made the decision." Eddie's response caused the smirk to disappear from Baughman's face. The fight may have been taken out of him because of his fatigue, and because of the lack of water, but his spunk still was with him.

Giving his prisoner another moment to rest, Baughman smiled over the spunk the Confederate soldier had displayed. He liked that in a man. "Reb, you're darn tootin'! We sure did get our butts handed to us at both places. Reckon old Bobby Lee really did give it to us at Fredericksburg like you say, but those days are over as you can see by what happened here today. Let me ask you another question. Again, I mean no disrespect to you or to your fellow soldiers by asking this of you. Tell me, why are all of ya fighting in this here war anyhow? Ya ain't got but a slim chance of winning this here fight. Why don't you cotton pickers just all go home so we can put this here war behind us? Personally, I don't give a hoot if y'all have slaves or not."

Eddie was tired, but he stewed over being called a cotton picker by the Yankee sergeant. Now he came back at him. "It ain't about slavery for me, Billy Yank, and I sure ain't no dang cotton picker like ya think I is! I'm fighting to keep yer darn intrudin' government out of Alabama, that's why I'm fighting in this here war. Same reason why South Carolina and Georgia boys are fightin' against ya. We don't need you folks tellin' us how to live our lives! I'm fightin' for Alabama, and fer my rights!"

"What rights are those, Reb?"

Eddie thought for a moment before realizing he was simply too tired to carry on the talk he was having with this soldier for much longer. "Same darn rights you is fightin' for, Billy Yank! We's all from the same country, least we were at one time. I'm fightin' for the same rights as y'all are, includin' the right to be left alone! No disrespect to y'all, but I'm too dang tired, too dang hungry, and too dang ticked off about what happened here today to talk with y'all any longer. Do what ya got to do with me, and let's get it over with!"

******

Over the next hour, Eddie, and the survivors of the 15th Alabama, some wounded, and others who had been simply taken prisoner, were herded up the hill to be guarded by several Union soldiers. Later they were marched off to be added to the growing number of prisoners that the Union had captured over the last two days. They would soon be fed a few meager bits of food, and given some water to drink, but for many of them it would be a long first few days as Union prisoners. For some of them, the lucky ones who survived the fighting without being injured, the war was over. For many others, especially for those soldiers who now were either wounded or sick in one way or another, they would soon succumb in prison due to their health issues. For those who had been injured in the brutal fighting, but who had escaped being captured, they would die where they had secreted themselves while hiding from Union soldiers who sought to take them prisoner. They had hid themselves within the rocks and boulders at Devil's Den, and in other places as well. There they would die from their injuries.

During this war neither side had much sympathy for enemy soldiers who had been captured or wounded. It was already proving especially difficult for both sides to just have enough to care for their own wounded during these first two days of the battle. With few doctors, few supplies, and with far too little medicine, both armies were ill-prepared to handle the thousands of men who had been injured in the fighting.

Unlike his cousin, Eddie Russell would spend the rest of the war in a Union prison camp. Poorly fed, and often in ill health during his confinement, he would barely survive the war. By the time it ended, he had lost nearly fifty pounds. For the rest of his life, he would never forget the hunger he had experienced during that dreadful period of time.

******

In the hours that followed the battle, just like the others who had been chased off of Little Round Top, soldiers of the 15th Alabama fought to find their way back to their regiments, and to the safety of the Confederate line. Like many of his men, Oates had scrambled over the top of Round Top to make his way back to safety. It would be a painful retreat that he would remember the rest of his life. Not only had he fled Little Round Top a defeated man, but he had been forced to leave his dead and wounded there as well. One of those that he had been forced to leave behind was his brother, Lt. John A. Oates, who had been mortally wounded during the fighting that day.

The 15th Alabama, just like the rest of the Confederate army, would soon fight again. The following day, on orders from General Lee, the Confederate army would again use a frontal attack to attack the Union line. The thousands of Confederate soldiers who fought on Day Three would fight with the same pride and determination as their brother soldiers had displayed on Little Round Top the previous day. They would just not fight with as many men as their army had within their ranks at the start of Day Two. As it was with other companies, as it was with other regiments, and as it was with other Corps, both North and South, the 15th Alabama would live to fight again, but with fewer men than they had when the previous day's battle started. The hill they had fought on was small in size, but the 15th Alabama had paid a deadly price to fight there.

13

War Brings a New Friendship.

"Too bad! Too bad! Oh! Too bad!"

General Robert E. Lee, C.S.A. – July 4th, 1863 - Gettysburg

The following day the 20th Maine rested in the early morning hours as they manned both Round Top and Little Round Top. Most of the seriously injured men had already been taken to various field hospitals behind the Union lines for care. Those who had sustained relatively minor injuries had already returned to the line. All of them now hoped and prayed for a quiet day.

Resting along the line, and in the shade that several maple trees provided, William saw Colonel Chamberlain walking amongst the men. As he watched, he saw Chamberlain stop to talk to the groups of men that manned the lookout posts on top of Round Top. Some he spoke to rather quietly as he tried to reassure them that all would be fine this day. With others, he simply nodded his head on occasion as he listened to what his men had to say. Others he spoke with made him laugh, and his comments in return made the men laugh as well. William could not help but smile as he watched his colonel move about the groups of men. He knew what Chamberlain was doing was being done out of genuine concern for those he commanded.

Walking to where William rested with a few other men as they watched out over the valley for any Confederate troop movements, Chamberlain stopped several feet away at first so he did not interrupt the conversation that was taking place. Waiting for the right moment, he finally addressed the small group of men. "Men, I hope you are all well this fine morning! You all deserve to be recognized for your efforts yesterday! Maine, and the entire army, just as I am, are all both very proud of you!" Waiting a brief moment before he spoke again, Chamberlain looked directly at William. "And how are you this fine morning, Sgt. Barton?"

Confused, William looked at his friends for an explanation. His puzzled look drew laughter from the others who had been sitting with him. They all had already heard the good news before he had. Other soldiers nearby broke out in smiles as they also knew what was taking place.

"Sir?" It was all William could think of to say as he started to stand up.

"I said, 'Good Morning, Sgt. Barton'." Even Chamberlain smiled at the confused look on William's face.

"Sir, I'm sorry, I . . . ."

Chamberlain continued to smile at William's confusion for a few more moments before telling him the good news. "I saw how you fought yesterday, and I liked what I saw. On a couple of occasions I saw you helping a few other men who, in the confusion of the moment we were facing, had rammed in two or more rounds into their muskets. I liked how you helped them stay calm. More importantly, I liked how you stayed calm. We need that kind of calmness displayed when we are fighting. Unfortunately we lost a few men yesterday, a few sergeants as well. What we lost has been replaced somewhat by those men from the 2nd Maine who have joined us. That said, I've taken the steps necessary to have you promoted to sergeant; should be official in a couple of days. Congratulations, sergeant!"

Surprised by what had unexpectedly happened to him, William's next comment drew laughter from Chamberlain, and from those who had been sitting around with him. "Thank you, sir! At least I think I thank you, sir."

After a round of backslaps and congratulatory handshakes from the others, Chamberlain and William took a brief walk. Quietly, and casually, they walked to the edge of Round Top. Pausing there, they each looked out over the once lush valley that now had been torn up by the brutal fighting that had taken place there.

"It's a beautiful view, William, but I'm afraid it's a view that has been stained for eternity due to the death and misery that has occurred here."

"I guess it has been, colonel. From what I've heard, I guess the fighting was pretty intense across the whole valley yesterday."

"That it was. I heard this morning that so much blood was spilled here yesterday that it made that little creek down there, Plum Run I believe the locals call it, made it run red with blood for a while yesterday afternoon. From what I saw yesterday, I wouldn't doubt that it actually happened. It wasn't a pretty sight to see, was it?"

"No, sir, that it wasn't."

Both men stood silent for a few moments as they thought of the number of soldiers who had died along the valley yesterday.

"William, I also heard that some of our boys have already taken to calling this place the Valley of Death. It's a cruel name for such a beautiful place, but I reckon it's a fitting name for it seeing what all happened here."

Reflecting on what Chamberlain had said to him, William stood quiet for a few moments before speaking again. "Let's hope that unpleasant name fades away with time, colonel."

Soon getting back to the business of the day, Chamberlain spoke again to his new sergeant. "William, I mean Sgt. Barton, I have your first assignment for you."

Chamberlain then explained to William that he wanted him, along with two soldiers of William's own choosing, to carefully crisscross the slopes of Little Round Top looking for any weapons, any ammunition, and anything of value that the 20th Maine might have left behind after yesterday's battle. "Most importantly, I want you to make sure we have not left anyone behind. Keep your eyes open out there for any Confederate snipers, but I want you to make sure our men have all been accounted for. If you find anything we can use, you have my permission to bring it back to the line. Take that wagon over yonder on Little Round Top, and fill it with whatever you find. Understand, sergeant?"

"Sir, yes, sir!"

******

William grabbed a protesting Harlow Dunbar, and a still very tired Albert Moody, to assist him with his first assignment. Moving the wagon closer to the base of Little Round Top, the three soldiers began the climb up the steep slope of the hill to look for whatever their outfit might need. As they walked, they carried their muskets with them in the event they ran into trouble.

"We ain't gonna get shot by some Confederate sniper trying to get back at us for yesterday is we?" Harlow Dunbar was very nervous as he walked in and around the still present bodies of many soldiers from the 15th and 47th Alabama regiments. "With my luck, one of these Johnny Rebs is faking that he's dead and he's just waiting for some fools like us to come walkin' through here."

"Hope not, Private!" William's reply was meant as a joke, and the three friends gave the comment a good laugh. The laughter helped to calm them all down as they were all somewhat uneasy over walking around the many dead bodies that still littered the slopes of the two hills.

Stopping to look at the grounds of the small but steep hill, William decided they needed a place to start their search. "Let's start over on the slope where those boys made their last charge yesterday. That's as good a place to start as any, I guess. We'll work our way back this way as we go."

"Yes, sir, sergeant!" William's two friends teased him back regarding his recent promotion. They were both pleased for him as he was one of the best soldiers they had been in the army with.

Scouring the slopes of Round Top, in the area where the 15th Alabama had retreated through the previous day, the men picked up a few rifles, three bayonets, and several cartridge belts. Each of the cartridge belts, like the several canteens they had found, was empty. They each knew that the lack of ammunition, and the absence of water, had played a factor in the outcome of the battle yesterday. A few more rounds of ammunition, some water, and some more men, might have had an impact on how the battle turned out yesterday. If they had all been available to the 15th Alabama yesterday they knew the Union's left flank might have collapsed, and things might have turned out very badly for their side. They were grateful the day had turned out like it did.

After scouring the slopes of Round Top, William and his two friends made their way back towards the positions they had held along the line the previous day. Walking several paces out in front of the others, and closer to the crest of Little Round Top, William saw several more dead soldiers from both the 15th and 47th Alabama regiments. Some were grossly disfigured from the intense fighting that had occurred, while others were now in the various stages of rigor mortis that had set in. Other bodies he saw had already started to bloat from the heat and humidity. Quickly he tried to complete his assignment as he navigated amongst the dead bodies, and the large boulders that were present. As he did, he also saw that many trees had been shattered from yesterday's gunfire. The damage to these trees was significant. As he scoured the hill, the awful smell that came from the piles of dead bodies was beginning to cause him to feel sick to his stomach.

Having retrieved several additional canteens and bayonets, as well at two Enfield rifles, William started to move downhill when he spied a saber lying on the ground near a dead Confederate officer. Stopping to pick up the trophy that was about to become his, he was startled to hear a weak voice call out to him. Reacting to the unexpected voice, he dropped everything he had collected. Quickly he searched to find the voice that had called out to him; it had nearly scared him to death. Frantically his eyes scanned the side of the hill to see who had scared him so.

"Please, please help me! Please, I'm hurt. Help me!"

William looked down to see a young Confederate soldier lying on the ground behind him. The injured soldier was lying on his back with his feet pointed back up the hill towards where the Union line had been yesterday. Two other Confederate soldiers had fallen dead on top of him; both had been killed after being struck several times by Union musket fire.

"Will you help me, sir? Please, I beg of you! I'm hurt kinda bad."

"Harlow! Albert! Get your butts over here, quick!" Looking around at first, William first checked to make sure he wasn't falling into some kind of a trap so he could be taken prisoner by a group of nearby

Confederate soldiers. Quickly he could tell that the other nearby soldiers had all been dead for a period of time, all victims of yesterday's battle.

Pulling on the right pant leg of one of the dead soldiers, William had the first body pulled off the injured soldier by the time Harlow and Albert arrived.

"What'd ya find, William?" Exhausted from their sprint up the steep slope, neither man saw the eyes of the injured Confederate soldier staring at them as they caught their breath.

"That there soldier is still alive! He just spoke to me." After dragging the first dead soldier away a few more feet, William pointed down at the injured soldier lying on the ground.

Thinking his friend was kidding him, Harlow at first didn't believe what he had heard. Then the injured soldier let out a cry of pain as William dragged the second dead soldier off of him. "Well, I'll be darn! He is still alive, ain't he?"

Taking a look at his friend at first, and then down at the injured soldier, William threw a sarcastic shot back at Harlow. "Dead men usually don't talk or cry out in pain, Harlow, at least none of the ones I've seen haven't!"

Kneeling down to see what injuries the young soldier had sustained, William saw he had been shot in the upper right shoulder, and that he apparently had also sustained what appeared to be a bayonet wound to his left hip. Examining the wounds closer, he let the soldier know what he saw. "Looks like a minie ball went clean through your shoulder. The bayonet wound looks worse than the gunshot wound to me. Surprised ya ain't bled out from these wounds, lying here as long as ya have been. You're a lucky man!"

After helping William get the injured soldier up into a sitting position against a medium sized boulder, Albert gave him a drink of water from his wooden canteen. "Here ya go, Johnny! Take a couple of small sips to start with." The drink of water received a friendly nod of appreciation. It was quickly followed by an obvious statement.

"I guess I'm the easiest prisoner y'all ever had to capture, huh? Seeing how y'all got me surrounded and all, I guess I ain't escaping from ya!" The injured soldier's comment caused William to briefly laugh as it was obvious this soldier couldn't have escaped from them even if he had wanted to.

Realizing that the soldier had tried to find some humor in the situation that was now confronting him, William decided to play along with him. "I guess you're right, Johnny. You now can consider yourself an official prisoner of the United States government! Don't try nothin' cause we got you surrounded like you said." William's comments caused the soldier to smile up at him, but neither Harlow nor Albert had figured out the comments had been made in jest. Both of them stood off to the side with serious looks on their faces.

Still smiling over what William had said to him, the injured soldier started to feel somewhat better after the two bodies had been pulled off of him. After taking another sip of water, the soldier handed the small canteen back to Albert. "Mighty grateful to y'all for helping me out! Mighty grateful! I'm hurt real bad, feel kinda busted up inside, might have a couple of broken ribs from those two fellas landing on me like they did. Between my shoulder being shot up, and these busted ribs, that's why I couldn't get them boys off of me all night. Did a bunch of hollerin' for help, but nobody come to help me. I know'd that someone heard me as I heard some soldier yell at me last night to stop all the yellin' I was doing. Finally got tired and fell asleep as I was plumb tuckered out from too much marching and fightin', and not enough eatin' and drinkin'. Kinda afraid to have done so as I weren't too sure I was gonna wake up." Taking a brief moment to catch his breath, the injured soldier spoke again. "That one soldier there, that red haired boy, that's my cousin. Private William J. Holloway was his name; lived in Macon County. He belonged to the 15th Alabama, Company G. A good man, a real good man! I suspect there's many a good man, from both sides of the fight, lying out here. Too bad, far too bad, if y'all ask me."

As Harlow knelt down next to the injured soldier, he did his best to stem the small amount of blood that still was flowing out of the soldier's right shoulder wound. Finished with his work, he asked the soldier what regiment he had been with. "15th Alabama, part of Longstreet's Corps. A good unit we was, and hopefully still are. Looking around I see we lost a bunch of boys yesterday, not telling how many are still left. Hate to see the boys lying like they are. Just ain't right!"

A strange silence existed between the men for a few moments as they all surveyed the hillside, and thought of those soldiers who weren't going home. Pushing himself up into a more comfortable position, the injured soldier asked Harlow the same question. "Who y'all with? What I mean is what outfit y'all fightin' with?"

"20th Maine. Colonel Chamberlain, the officer that ordered the bayonet charge at you fellas yesterday, he's our commanding officer."

"Brave man he must be to have dun ordered that charge, brave or foolish, I reckon. I'll tell ya that we even dun heard that order rumble across your line yesterday. I'd be lying to y'all if I didn't tell ya that hearing the word bayonet being yelled scared me some. Didn't like the thought then about being stuck by one of your boys using his bayonet on me, and I still don't like the thought now. One of your boys got me in the hip with one I guess, never even seen it coming. Too many soldiers running each and every way for me to see everything being thrown my way. Maybe it were a good thing I didn't see it coming, might have gotten stuck even worse than I did if I seen it coming. 20th Maine, you say, huh? Can't say I ever heard of y'all before now; guess I likely will from now on though. Y'all gave us a fair whippin' yesterday."

Albert and Harlow smiled at the compliment the injured soldier directed at their regiment, but William showed no emotion. "You boys fought well yesterday too! Coming up that hill like ya did. I know I counted at least five times ya came at us. Last night, for what's it all worth to ya, we gave you boys a heap of credit for keeping on like ya did. Your regiment's a credit to your state, and to your army, that's for sure!" Both of his friends nodded their heads in agreement at what William had just said about their adversary's ability to fight. The comment caused a weak and tired Louis to smile. He hadn't expected his foes to pay his regiment a compliment after they had killed so many Union soldiers.

"Much obliged, fellas. Nice to hear other soldiers complimenting ya on your fightin' ability. Seems strange to hear it from all of ya though as we's were trying to kill y'all!" The comment drew a nervous kind of laughter from each of the four men as they each thought it over in their heads. "Fellas, can y'all get me back to my line or to one of our hospitals? I need to get some help for these injuries I got. I'm feelin' poorly!"

As the injured soldier finished speaking, in the distance the exchange of angry artillery fire could be heard for the first time that day. It lasted for several minutes before pausing. Each of the men exchanged excited looks between themselves.

"Something's started to stir for the day. We ain't gonna try and get ya to your lines as likely some of your boys will try to shoot our heads off or something like that, but we'll get ya some help. We ain't gonna leave ya out here alone." After directing Harlow and Albert to collect what they had found, and to make their way back to the wagon, William knelt down next to his prisoner.

"Listen here, Johnny Reb, this is likely gonna hurt some, but I'm gonna pick ya up and carry ya over to the wagon. I'm probably gonna get my butt chewed on some for doing this, but I ain't gonna leave ya out here to die. Gotta have some concern for ya, even if ya do talk kinda funny!" Then being as careful as he could, William lifted the injured soldier off the ground.

As he carried his prisoner to the waiting wagon, William was asked why he was doing this for not only a stranger, but for an enemy soldier as well. "I promised my father that I would always try to act like he raised me, as a Christian. I'm far from perfect, and my father is a better Christian than I am, or likely ever will be, but I'm trying to do better. I'm kind of hoping ya might agree with me!"

"I'd praise ya even more than I already am, Billy Yank, but these busted up ribs of mine are killing me some. Just know I appreciate what y'all have dun for me, even if it does lead to me spending the rest of the war in some Yankee prisoner of war camp."

******

The wagon that carried William and the others soon pulled up outside a field hospital that was located to the rear of the Union line, one not too far from Spangler's Spring. Flags mounted in the ground told them they had reached the location where the Eleventh Corps had set up a hospital of some sort. Situated around the outside of a large nearby wooden barn were two overflowing large white tents that served as part of the makeshift hospital for Union soldiers who had been injured in a variety of different ways. The barn itself was being used as a place to house those soldiers who had already been treated for their wounds. Inside the tents, soldiers were being treated for all sorts of wounds and injuries they had sustained in the first two days of fighting. The smaller of the two tents was also being used as an operating room by several different Union surgeons. While the cries that came from the injured within the barn, and from within the largest of the two tents, were difficult to listen to, the cries and moans that came from the smaller tent were especially painful to listen to. Despite the best efforts of the surgeons, it was easy to tell that good things were not happening inside the tent to the soldiers who were being cared for. To the rear of the tents, William could see that the remains of several dead soldiers had been laid out on the ground. The dead had been partially covered with an assortment of canvass tarps, blood soaked sheets that were once white, and blankets. The growing pile of bodies had made it easy to see what the medical staff had tried to cover from view. Next to the remains were two piles of arms and legs that Union surgeons had amputated in attempts to save the lives of many injured soldiers. The piles he saw made William want to gag as they now made the bloody fighting he had been a part of seem even more real. Staring at the two piles caused him to stand still for several moments, and his lengthy stare caused Albert and Harlow to pick up on what it was that he was staring at. They also quickly grew mortified over what they saw. The hot humid air around the tents was stale and calm and the smell of death seemed to hover nearby. It was the most depressing area that the three men had ever seen.

Close to where the bodies had been laid out, William saw a third tent that had been set up as well. It had once been white, but the canvass tent was now stained with both blood and dirt from being used far too many times already in the war. It was not as big in size as the other two that he had seen, and it was one that displayed a small white and red painted sign on one of the tent poles. Being careful not to step on the injured soldiers lying on the ground, he moved closer so he could see what the sign read. Written in big red letters was *"Dr. Thomas Jenkins, Embalming Surgeon"*. Inside the tent, on a folding table of some kind were the laid out remains of a Union officer. The undressed body had been partially covered with a white sheet. The thought of what was occurring during this medical procedure caused a chill to run down William's back.

Outside the large tents, William and his friends continued to hear several Union soldiers screaming out in pain from the injuries they had sustained. Nearby, they saw three other soldiers lying on makeshift cots, their traumatic head wounds bandaged by blood stained rags that at one time were white in color. Not a sound came from these three soldiers as they patiently waited for either help or death to come their way.

Walking closer to the front of the largest tent, its flaps pulled back so fresh air could flow through it; William could hear the cries and sobs of other injured soldiers as they were being cared for. No matter how hard he tried, he could not ignore the calls for help from the many soldiers that were there. Injured men littered the area just outside the tent as well, some missing arms and legs, many suffering from stomach and head wounds of all types. Looking down at some of the men who now were missing legs and arms, he could not ignore the many bandaged, but still bleeding stumps he saw. Blood soaked the ground in several areas in and around the outside of the large tent. The bloody stumps he saw were places where arms and legs had recently been attached. They were extremities their owners had just taken for granted they would always have. War had sadly changed that for far too many people.

As he collected himself from the horrors of war that he had just seen, William spied a nearby doctor who had just left one of the tents to compose himself. He had spent several hours hacking off the arms and legs of Union soldiers in attempts to save their lives, and had treated countless others for a variety of wounds and injuries that he never would have imagined seeing during his medical career. After working desperately to keep up with the pace that the injured were arriving at, the doctor had walked out of the tent to take a brief break from the misery he had been treating. The front of his shirt, his hands, his pants, and his once brown colored boots, were stained with the blood of the many soldiers he had frantically tried to help. Tired from working for many hours without much rest, and shaken by what he had seen during those hours, the doctor's hands had trembled as he lit his cigar. Leaning against a split rail fence, he had just taken his first puff when William spoke to him.

"Doc, beg your pardon, but we need some help over here!"

Walking with William over to the wagon, Doctor Jeffrey Brandau soon saw the injured soldier lying in the back of the wagon. Quickly he saw the grey uniform that the soldier was wearing. "You need to take him over to where the other Rebs are waiting to be treated. We're only working on our guys right now."

William grabbed Doc Brandau's arm as he turned to walk back to work within the large tents. "Doc, but this man's hurt. He needs your help!"

Pausing to wipe the perspiration off of his forehead with his shirt's dirty left sleeve, Brandau tried to apologize for not being able to help, but was cut off in mid-sentence by William.

"Doc, ya got family fightin' in this war?"

William's question caught the doctor off-guard, but he soon answered the question. "Yes, I have. Both of my brothers are serving on General Grant's staff. I believe they are down near Vicksburg as we speak. Why do you ask?"

Standing near the rear of the wagon, Harlow and Albert, along with their injured prisoner, all wondered where William was going with his line of questioning.

"They both in good health, Doc?"

Again Doc Brandau was confused by William's questioning, and like the others he also wondered where this was going. "Yes, soldier, they are. At least as far as I know they are."

"That's good, Doc, real good. I'm sure that brings great comfort to your ma, knowing that her boys are all well. My ma is gonna be real upset with me if I don't get some medical care for my cousin here."

The news that the injured Confederate soldier in the wagon was related to the Union soldier he was talking with startled Doc Brandau, and his eyes bounced back and forth from the injured soldier to William. Pausing to try to figure out how two soldiers that were wearing distinctly different uniforms could be related, Brandau took another couple of puffs on his cigar before speaking again. "This soldier is related to you? I can see that you're from Maine, at least that's where

I believe your regiment is from, so how can this Confederate soldier be your cousin?" The look in Brandau's face doubted the sincerity of what he had been told.

Without missing a beat, William countered the Brandau's verbal challenge to him. "Doc, with all due respect, people come and go all over this here country of ours all the time, my family included. Last I knew, I even got kin living in Kansas of all places. Lord knows why, but I do. I ain't got neither the time nor the inclination to map out all of my family's wanderings for ya right now, but I'm telling ya this man's my cousin. I'm asking ya to see past whatever it is ya want to believe, and to also see past the differences in the colors of our uniforms so ya can help my cousin with his injuries. I know my ma and her sister both would be downright grateful to ya for your assistance. Can ya do that for us?"

Doc Brandau's eyes again bounced back and forth from the injuries he saw and William's face for a few seconds. "What the heck! One more injured soldier isn't going to make that much of a difference. No disrespect to your cousin, but because of the color of his uniform it would be best if you set him up outside over yonder. Best cover up that uniform of his with a blanket or something. One of our boys might take exception to him being here with the boys in blue, if you know what I mean. I'll come out and tend to him shortly."

As William extended his right hand to shake hands with Brandau, an injured Alabama soldier breathed a sigh of relief. Help was on the way, even if it was coming in the shape of a Yankee doctor.

******

The intensity of the cannon fire picked up as William, with Harlow's help, placed the injured soldier on a hospital cot at the far side of one of the hospital tents. He was the only Confederate soldier near the tents. Quickly they covered his grey colored uniform with two blankets they had found on Little Round Top.

As Harlow and Albert walked back to their wagon, William paused for a moment to speak to his prisoner for one last time. "Well, I guess that's it, Johnny Reb! I wish ya well and all. Give a thought to what we dun for ya the next time ya come across one of our boys that's been injured. I'm expecting ya to do that for me!"

Painfully pushing himself up off the ground, the Alabama soldier rested in a somewhat reclined position until his momentary flash of intense pain subsided. "I sure do appreciate y'all gettin' me some help for my injuries like ya dun. I promise I'll be glad to help one of your boys along the line some place. I owe ya that at least. Ya know, I heard all of you Yankees were a bunch of liars and cheaters, but I never thought I'd come to appreciate it. Why'd ya lie to the doc like ya did? We ain't kin. Heck, I ain't even got to know your name yet! Why'd ya do it for me?"

William knelt down next to his injured prisoner, and smiled a big grin. "I told ya before; my daddy's a good Christian man. I'm trying to catch up to him, that's all. Ya probably would have done the same for me."

"I'm not so sure I would have. My daddy raised me not to lie to others!" Both men gave a quick laugh at the joke the injured Alabama soldier had offered. It was one that William continued to smile over for a few moments. As he did, the sound of cannon fire could again be heard.

"Well, Johnny Reb, I've got to go. By the sound of them cannons I hear, it sounds like something is gonna happen today. I best get ready for it. William Barton, that's my name. What's yours?"

"Louis Hiram Pierce. I'm from Russell County, Alabama. How about y'all?"

"We're Maine boys, all of us. As we told ya, we're part of the 20th Maine."

Falling back on his cot due to the pain he was experiencing, Louis looked up at William. "Ya didn't tell me where in Maine y'all are from."

Standing up to leave, William looked over at his two friends who were waiting impatiently in the wagon as he pointed to them. "Albert, he's the one driving the wagon; he's from a place called Waldoboro. My other buddy, Harlow, he hails from a small place called Nobleboro. Come to think of it, Old Harlow, he's about everything but noble!"

William's joke about Harlow caused Louis to flash a big grin across his sweaty dirty face. "He's a good man, ain't he?"

"Harlow? Yep, he's that and more. So's Albert! Me, I'm a Portland man. I work in my pa's boatyard near Portland Harbor, just off a street called Commercial Street. Portland's a fine little town, can't wait to get back there. Hope it's soon!"

"Billy Yank, y'all take care of yourself! I'm grateful to all of ya for your kind help. It's a pleasure to have met ya, even if you are a Yank! I wish y'all, especially you, a safe journey through the rest of this miserable war. Take care of yourself, ya hear?"

Talking to Louis helped convince William that the only difference between his Confederate prisoner and his own friends was an imaginary line that separated the North from the South. He realized Louis was someone he probably would have liked to have as a friend back home.

"I hear ya, Johnny Reb, I hear ya! Take good care of yourself as well. I doubt we'll ever see each other again as Alabama is a heck of a journey north to where I'm at, but who knows. I hope ya make it home safe!" William gave a final nod to Louis and then turned to walk back to where his friends were waiting for him. As he started to walk away, Louis called out to him for the last time.

"William!"

Pausing before he climbed aboard the wagon, William looked back at Louis, and saw he had once again raised himself off the ground.

"God bless you! I won't forget what y'all have done for me. Thank you, sir!"

The loud roar of a nearby Union artillery battery caused William to turn away from looking at Louis. Now he quickly climbed aboard the wagon. Looking back over his shoulder as Albert drove the wagon away, he turned and gave his new friend a final quick wave.

The brief meeting that day between the two opposing soldiers would be a story they both would tell for many years to come. It was a meeting that in later years would help to start the healing between the two sides.

14

SURRENDER.

*" . . . . officers and men paroled . . . . arms and materiel surrendered . . .
not to include officer's side-arms . . . let all men who claim to own a horse
or mule take the animals home with them."*

PRESIDENT LINCOLN TO GENERAL GRANT REGARDING SOME
OF THE TERMS OF THE CONFEDERATE SURRENDER.

The fighting that took place in and around Little Round Top, in
Devil's Den, in the Wheatfield, and along the Emmitsburg Road, had
been intense as it unfolded on Day Two. Many thought it could never
be equaled in its overall magnitude. They quickly would find out they
were wrong.

The attacks on Day Three, ones made by the Confederacy on the
Union defenses, primarily the attack that has come to be known as
Pickett's Charge, while they failed to accomplish their goals, certainly
equaled, if not exceeded, the brutality of the fighting of the previous
day. The number of dead and wounded that littered the battlefield from
these two previous days was already a staggering number. The number
of soldiers who would die fighting on Day Three would make the total
number of deaths one that is still difficult to comprehend even to this
day. The losses would impact both armies, primarily the South, in the
months to come.

Gettysburg will long be remembered as one of the turning points in
the war for the North. As news of the events there unfolded and became
known to the American people, through the heroic efforts of the men
who fought and died there, and from the brief speech President Lincoln
gave there in November, 1863, the names of Meade, Reynolds, Buford,
Chamberlain, Lee, Longstreet, Pickett, Oates, and many others, would

become well-known. So would many of the locations where brave men from both sides of the war had fought and died. Unlike so many other battles, specific locations at Gettysburg, ones like Little Round Top, the Peach Orchard, Culp's Hill, and many other similar sites, easily became associated with the battle that took place there. They are locations that will be long remembered by the American people as far too many of our brave forefathers died fighting there for us to ever be able to forget what took place in that small little town.

******

As the Battle of Gettysburg came to a close, both armies, first the Confederate army, and then the North, began to move back south. As the Confederates began their orderly retreat on July 4th, in the first of several days of rain, they did so to reorganize and to resupply themselves once they retreated into the relative safety of the Shenandoah Valley. They just had to first make it safely across the Potomac River.

The Union army, in pursuit of the beaten Confederate army, harassed them for days, but only half-heartedly. Like they had in the past on many occasions, the Union army again failed to seize an opportunity they were given. It was an opportunity to deal Lee's crippled and pinned down army a devastating and, perhaps, final blow.

The slow moving Confederate wagon trains, while attacked off and on by Union forces, soon found themselves trapped between the swollen Potomac River and the Union army. They were ready to be finished off, but Meade initially elected not to attack them in force. Days later when the Union army finally decided to attack them harder than they had, Lee and his army were across the river and gone. Not pursuing Lee, as Lincoln had wanted Meade to do, not only allowed the Army of Northern Virginia to escape, but failing to destroy a wounded enemy allowed them time to heal and regroup. Doing so tragically extended the war for many more months. The failure to destroy the Confederate army when they had a chance to do so or to devastate them even more than they already were, and possibly even passing on an opportunity to capture Lee himself, would cost both armies the lives of thousands of more men.

Included in the moves of both armies out of Gettysburg were the movements of both the 20th Maine and the 15th Alabama. Like their respective armies, they were beaten up from the fighting that had occurred there.

******

As General Lee, and his Army of Northern Virginia, retreated back into the safety of the Shenandoah Valley, other bad news, equally as bad as the news of Lee's losses at Gettysburg, soon spread out across the South. While perhaps not as significant in the amount of material, and in the number of losses of men, the news of Vicksburg and Port Hudson both falling to Union forces did little to bolster the morale of the southern populace. Additional news of other losses in the Tullahoma Campaign, one led by General Braxton Bragg, soon followed.

While the defeat at Gettysburg was a significant one for the South, no one really could predict how the battle would rank in its overall importance at the time as the war was still a work in progress. However, it was, when combined with the news of other recent losses, all bad news for the South, principally the news related to the losses at Gettysburg and Vicksburg. While not spelling the end of the Confederacy, the news of these defeats had a devastating effect on the morale within the Confederate armies, and with the people of the South. Soon cries began to rise across the Confederacy, including ones from many newspapers and prominent citizens in North Carolina, for peace talks to commence with the North. These were similar cries to the ones that had recently echoed across the North.

Learning that some of the criticism had been directed at him, some of it related to the tactics he had employed at Gettysburg, Lee offered to resign his position in August, 1863, but it was not accepted. Despite his loss at Gettysburg, he still retained the faith and confidence of President Jefferson Davis, and of a large majority of the southern population.

While the Confederate losses had a negative impact in the South, the opposite quickly happened in the North. Northern newspapers, some correctly, and some with stories that falsely trumpeted the pending surrender of the Confederacy, ran stories of the great Union victories that had occurred. Morale and support of the war, that had reached all-time lows after Union losses at Fredericksburg and Chancellorsville, now soared. Cries of joy soon replaced most of the negative opinion in the North. News from Gettysburg, and then from Vicksburg, had quickly changed all of that.

******

The 20th Maine would fight in the war until the surrender of Lee's army, in April, 1865, at Appomattox Court House. Between Gettysburg and Appomattox, the 20th Maine would fight at the Battle of the Wilderness, at Globe Tavern, at Five Forks, at Dabney's Mills, and on many other battlefields across the South.

The 15th Alabama would also fight in many more battles. They would fight in the Battle of Chickamauga, at the Battle of Browns Ferry, at the Battle of Bean's Station, and also during the Army of Tennessee's Knoxville Campaign. They would also fight, like the 20th Maine, at the Battle of Spotsylvania Court House, at the Battle of Cold Harbor, during the Siege of Petersburg, and during the Appomattox Campaign.

The valiant efforts of many soldiers from both regiments would earn each of them everlasting fame in the history of the Civil War. In addition, several men from both regiments would win either the Union's Medal of Honor, or the South's similar honor, the Southern Cross of Honor, for acts of gallantry on the fields of battle.

For William Barton, the failure of his army to hurt the Confederate troops even more after Gettysburg would mean that he had many more battles to participate in and live through before the war would come to an end. From Gettysburg to Appomattox, he would be wounded three more times, but never too seriously. During that time he saw several of his friends killed, and others maimed and wounded, but he continued to persevere. Just as he had promised his father he would.

******

As word of a possible surrender grew stronger, a truce was put into effect by Grant and Lee. In the days before the truce began, it had become well understood that the war was about to end. Waiting for the official word to be heard, Chamberlain and his men, as did many other Union commands in the Appomattox area, began to collect the guns and ammunition that Confederate soldiers had abandoned along the various routes of travel near that small quiet town. As he helped to collect these items, a courier soon found Chamberlain and delivered a message to him. It was one that directed him to report to the nearby field headquarters.

At Appomattox Court House, General Joshua Chamberlain was assigned the honor of commanding the surrender of Confederate troops there. While given the order to do so by General Charles Griffin, the order to receive the flags and arms of the surrendering Army of Northern Virginia had come directly from General Ulysses S. Grant. After being ordered to Union HQ and learning of his assignment, Chamberlain left there in the early morning hours to begin to plan the surrender. In doing so, he quickly assembled the remnants of the Union's Fifth Corps. He wanted them to have the honor of being placed along the Union line near him when the surrender soon began. Among those soldiers from the Fifth Corps were the veterans of many battles. They were the men he had fought with for several years. They were men from Maine, Michigan, Pennsylvania, New York, and Massachusetts.

On the cold grey morning of April 12th, at around five in the morning, mounted on his horse to the right of where his men stood, Chamberlain sat ready to accept the surrender of the Confederate troops. With great anticipation, he soon watched as the Confederate army approached his position.

******

As he stood in the front row of the brigade, barely twenty feet away from Chamberlain and with the courthouse off to his left, William watched as the proud but beaten Confederate troops approached his position. As those troops approached the assembled formation of Union soldiers, a Union bugler sounded. Upon hearing Chamberlain's command, Sgt. William Barton, as did the rest of the 20th Maine, and as did the other Union soldiers who stood with them, came to attention, and saluted the Confederate soldiers as their regiments reached the surrender location. Chamberlain's men quietly rendered the salute to the vanquished men they had bitterly fought against for several years. They were not salutes that recognized these soldiers, or their officers, or their flags, but rather they were salutes that welcomed the members of the Confederate army back into the Union as the Confederacy now no longer existed. Leading the way for the Confederacy was Lt. General John B. Gordon. Shortly behind him were the battered remnants of Longstreet's Corp, and the Corps of men that had once belonged to Stonewall Jackson. Included were the divisions of soldiers that had been led by Generals Hood and Pickett. The war had reduced their numbers greatly.

Standing there as he watched the various divisions pass by, William kept a keen eye out for Louis Pierce. His eyes quickly scanned the ranks of men each time an Alabama flag passed by, hoping to briefly see the face of the only Confederate soldier he had gotten to know during the war. While soldiers such as A.N. Agerton, J.P. Ballard, Joseph Beel, and many others from the 15th Alabama passed by, Louis had not. "Did he die from the wounds I saw that day, or did he get killed in some other battle? Is he a prisoner in some camp, I wonder?" These were among the many thoughts and questions that raced through William's head after the long line of Confederate troops had passed by him that day. Of the 1,958 men who had comprised the 15th Alabama at the start of the war, only 172 men were able to answer Roll Call on the morning of the surrender. Like so many other regiments, the war had decimated the ranks of the 15th Alabama.

The surrender would take most of the day to complete as the long line of Confederate soldiers took hours to pass. Throughout the day, wagons and wagons of Confederate rifles, swords, battle flags, and other items were hauled away by Union soldiers. By day's end, over 15,000 muskets and rifles, along with seventy-two battle flags, had been surrendered.

Watching as the Confederate soldiers stacked their rifles and muskets in large piles, and seeing them as they placed their cartridge boxes in another separate but growing pile, William also watched as they placed their battle flags on the ground nearby. Watching this all unfold, he was taken aback by the number of soldiers who added bare flag staffs to the piles, their proud flags already secreted away so they could be brought home as reminders of the war. Other groups of men rushed forward to touch their flags one last time. With tears in their eyes, they knew the war was over and that they would never again see the flag they had fought for. Some soldiers rushed forward to grab their flags, tearing bits of the flag off to serve as keepsakes to take home. The small pieces of their cloth flags would serve as something to remember from the war. The sight of so many proud soldiers, each wanting a small piece of their regimental or state flags, caused William to glance up at the two flags he had helped to defend. He was as proud of those flags as the Confederate soldiers were of theirs.

While they were a beaten army, they were still a proud group of soldiers as they passed through Appomattox Court House that day. Finished with the surrender, the former soldiers of the Confederate army were paroled, and they prepared for their long walks home. While the bitter taste of defeat would linger with many of them for years, others would quickly move on with their lives. Each of them in some way would help start the healing process that the nation so desperately needed.

It was a healing process that had just barely started when it was interrupted by another terrible tragedy that quickly struck the nation. The brutal war had barely ended when President Lincoln was assassinated, on April 14th, at Ford's Theater, in Washington. Now the nation had two wounds to recover from. It would take years to do.

******

On Saturday, April 15th, the 20th Maine marched from Appomattox Court House to the South Side Railroad's Evergreen Station. Camping there for the night, they were up early the next morning and soon on the move to Washington, D.C. On July 16, 1865, the 20th Maine was formally mustered out of service of the Union army. Most of the war weary soldiers would quickly head for home by train.

Answering Lincoln's call for volunteers had cost the 20th Maine one hundred and fifty brave men. They also lost another one hundred and forty-six men to disease and illness, and had another three hundred and eighty-one men wounded during their service to the Union cause. Additionally, fifteen men from the regiment had served out the war in Confederate prison camps.

******

The 15th Alabama proudly served the Confederacy until the war's end. Paroled like other regiments from the Army of Northern Virginia, the 15th Alabama would never fight again. For Louis Pierce, he would not be at Appomattox with his brothers-in-arms. The war, and his fighting days, had painfully ended for him at Gettysburg.

15

Going Home!

"We had them in our grasp . . . . And nothing I could say or do could make the Army move."

President Abraham Lincoln describing General Meade's decision not to pursue a defeated Confederate army after Gettysburg.

After the 20th Maine had participated in the Union's Grand Review of the Army, in Washington, D.C., and after being mustered out of the army, William and his friends made their way back home.

******

Walking alone down Portland's Commercial Street gave William his first real sense that he had survived the long war. The warm sunny morning, and the smell of the fresh salt air as it gently blew in off the harbor, told him he was finally home. Seeing the sights of his hometown, including the fishing boats passing by in the harbor, and the many people who passed by him on the sidewalk, told him he was home. The war was over and he could now get on with his life. The sights he saw, and the thoughts he had of a more peaceful time before him, brought a pleasing smile to his face.

******

The large wooden door to the boathouse had been pushed open so fresh air could pass through the building on this warm sunny day. Sunlight streaming into the building through several large opened windows picked up traces of sawdust that momentarily lingered in the air. Pausing by the door, William could see a large rowboat had recently just been sanded. It sat patiently waiting for several fresh coats of paint to be applied to its hull.

Inside the boathouse, and just off to his left, William heard the noise of a saw as it was carefully being used to cut strips of wood for a new boat that was being built. Walking a few steps further inside, he saw his father working with his back turned to him. Seeing his father working brought a smile to his face and tears to his eyes. He truly had made it back home.

Waiting until his father had finished his sawing, William finally announced his presence. "Hello, Pa! I made it home! I'm back with all of my parts!"

The unexpected sound of William's voice startled Jacob Barton. Turning quickly to his left to first make sure the voice he had heard was his son's, he then ran to hug his son. For the first time since his son had been gone, Jacob shed tears. Unlike the last time he had cried, these were tears of a father's joy. His son had safely come home from the war.

"Let me look at ya, boy! It looks like ya grown another inch or two on me while ya was gone! Looks like you could use some of your ma's cookin' to put some weight back on ya. I suspect they didn't feed ya too well, huh? Ya seen her yet?"

Still beaming from his father's warm welcome, William wiped away his own tears with his left sleeve. "No, Pa, I ain't seen her yet. I came right here after gettin' off the train; wanted to see you first. I'm looking forward to some of her cookin' though. Been thinking about it since I left to be honest. The food we got most of the time was none too good. I'm ready for a good meal!"

"Whatcha got there, son? Some kind of sword it looks like, that yours?"

Picking up the sword from where he had set it down on the sawdust covered wooden floor with his haversack, and with his few other belongings, William handed it to his father.

"I brought this home for ya, Pa, got it at Little Round Top during the fightin' we dun at Gettysburg. Me and a few of the boys chased down a Reb officer when he was tryin' to get away from us. Son of a gun even slashed me a bit with it before he surrendered. He got me mad for doing that to me, but I held off on doing what I wanted to do to him. Wanted you to be proud of me, so I just punched him instead of killin' him." William spent the next few minutes telling his father about the fighting he had done at Gettysburg, and what he had seen there. The news of what his son had experienced alarmed Jacob, but he did his best to hold his emotions in check. He did not want his son to see the shock he was feeling after learning of the battle's brutality.

"Pa, I'll tell you more later! Even got a few more things to show ya from the war, but not now. I want to go see ma. It's been too long since I seen her!"

Jacob hugged his son again, holding the embrace for several moments. As he did, he silently thanked the Lord for bringing his son home safely. "Praise you, Lord, for listening to my prayers. Praise you!"

Letting go of his son, Jacob happily yelled out. "Let's go, William! We're gonna give ma a big surprise!"

******

William's mother had almost fainted when she saw her son walking home with her husband. Her many prayers had been answered as William had returned home safely from the war. It took her husband and son several minutes to finally calm her down. After spending a good hour asking her son about the war, she now refused to allow him to start back to work at the boatyard just after returning home. Talking to her husband, and her son, as they all sat around the small dinner table in their home, she let Jacob know her feelings quite strongly. "My boy is gonna rest for as long as he wants. I'm not having him going back to work so soon after just gettin' home! You've been doing just fine without him for all this time, another few days or so ain't gonna hurt nothing. You can just keep on doing whatever it is you're doing without him until he gets some rest! Ain't gonna hurt nothing having him just sitting home with me for a spell. I'm fixin' to feed my boy real well over the next few days! You too if ya don't cause me no problems while I'm fussin' over my boy! Ya hear me?" Barbara Barton playfully smiled at her husband as she finished speaking. Jacob and William were her whole life, and she loved taking care of them by attending to all of their needs. Within another few minutes, she had her small kitchen buzzing as she worked to cook her son his first good meal in months.

William laughed at the strong position his mother had taken, and smiled at the amusement he saw in his father's face after listening to his wife speak to him like that. It had been unusual for his mother to have talked so sternly to her husband like that, but he knew he held a special place in his mother's heart. He liked how she had jokingly stood her ground to his father. He also liked the fact that she would be baking some special treats for him in the coming days. He had missed her cooking terribly.

"Fair enough, Mother! Fair enough!" Jacob knew it was an argument that he didn't care to have, nor one he could have ever won. He simply chose to agree with his wife's position about William resting up from the war. "Better feed him good, it looks like the boy needs a few good meals."

******

Two weeks had passed since William had arrived back home in Portland. He had spent his time resting, eating his mother's fine cooking, and catching up with his friends in the area. He had even managed to sneak down to the boatyard on a couple of occasions without his mother knowing about it. The smell of fresh cut wood, the salt air flowing into the boathouse, and the smell of a freshly painted boat, helped to reinforce to him that life was becoming normal again.

Now a more confident person because of the many experiences he had lived through while in the army, William's increased confidence led him to begin to call on a girl he had known for years. The war had given him both confidence and maturity well beyond his years. The girl he had a fancy for had lived roughly four miles from his house in Portland for several years. He had come to know her from her family's lumber business, and from the same church their families had attended. He had always had a passing interest in her, but had always been somewhat shy about extending their relationship past the friendship stage. Now with almost three years having gone by since they had last seen each other, Ann Bennett had matured as well. The pretty blond haired girl he had known for years had now become a very attractive young woman. The feelings that William had for her, were similar to the ones that she had always had for him.

Finally rested and fattened up since returning home, and now with a pretty young lady he had started to court, William convinced his mother it was time to return to work. He had been anxious to do so as he knew getting back to work would distract his mind from the sights and sounds he had been recently having about the war.

In his first few days back at work, William had eased back into the boat building business by painting a new boat his father had just finished building for a local fisherman. It took him a few days to apply the several coats of paint, but it was a relatively simple task to complete. It was one that helped to ease him back into the boat business.

On his fourth day back at work, William had just finished applying the last coat of paint, and was admiring his work when he saw his father speaking with someone near the large wooden door to the boathouse. Cleaning up his work area near the back of the building, he looked up to see his father pointing in his direction. With little, if any, real interest, he watched as the person his father had finished speaking with began to walk towards him.

Still not paying too much attention to what was unfolding in the boathouse, as he was more concerned with getting most of the sticky black paint off of his hands, William was soon startled by the greeting he heard.

"Hey, Billy Yank! Ya remember me? Y'all better have cuz I dun come a long way to see ya!"

Looking up, William had to somewhat shield his eyes to see who had greeted him due to the bright sunlight flooding into the building through the boathouse windows. Moving a couple of steps to his right soon enabled him to see who it was that had greeted him. The long thin smiling face was easily recognizable and he quickly realized who it was that was speaking to him. It was a face he never thought he would ever see again. It was certainly one that he never would have thought he would see in Portland.

"Is that really you, Johnny Reb? Is that you, Louis? What in tarnation are ya doin' all the way up here in Maine? And, what in tarnation are ya doin' wearin' a Yankee kepi hat? Last I knew, you were fightin' on the other side!"

Smiles, hugs, and handshakes were exchanged between the two excited young men before another word was spoken. Off to the side, Jacob watched intently as the two former adversaries warmly greeted each other.

"Louis, the last I seen of you was when I left ya at the field hospital. I have wondered from time to time if ya had made it through the war, even looked for ya when your fellow Alabamians marched by me at Appomattox Courthouse. I was hopin' to see ya that day, but obviously I didn't. Scared me some when I didn't see ya as I wondered what might have happened to ya. But now I can't believe my favorite cousin is standing right here in front of me, alive and well at that! I'm tickled to see ya survived the war! It makes my heart feel real good!"

Both men laughed at William's reference to them being cousins, and they again embraced each other as they did. Their laughter continued even longer when they spoke about how William had tricked Doc Brandau into treating Louis for his injuries. "William, ya dun sure fooled the good doc that day!" After laughing for another few minutes, Louis explained why he was wearing the blue kepi hat. "Dun found it alongside a road in Maryland some place. Stuck it in my saddlebags here so I could put it on when I first seen ya, thought I'd try to get a laugh out of ya by doing so." Taking the hat off, Louis handed it to his friend. "Best ya take this from me, William. Folks back home won't take too kindly to me wearing this hat back there. The color blue ain't too well-thought-of these days, if ya know what I mean." William couldn't help but to agree with his friend's comments about the hat.

For several moments, William could not help but to stare at the blue hat his Confederate friend had given him. It had quickly brought back memories of wearing a similar hat. As he continued to stare at it, he saw it bore the insignia of a Union cavalry regiment. Finished staring at the hat, he formally introduced Louis to his father. After doing so, he again asked his friend what had caused him to be in Portland. It would prove to be an answer that made William's father quite proud.

"Came here to see you! Ya dun something very special for me, something that most soldiers would never have dun, especially for a soldier from the other side of the war. I knew the day y'all left me at the hospital that if I survived the war that I was coming here to see ya in Maine. I really didn't have the chance to properly thank ya for your help that day so I had to come. The doc treated my injuries, but you saved my life. I had to come, couldn't have lived with myself if I hadn't!"

Hearing the story of how his son and Louis had met, and how William had saved Louis' life, caused Jacob to smile. "I'm proud of what ya done for this here soldier, William! Very proud!"

"He's a good man, Mr. Barton! A real good man! I'll never forget what he dun for me. Ya know, he joked with me that day when I asked him why he dun it, helped save my life and all. Know what he told me? Told me he'd dun it because of you! Told me y'all wuz a good Christian man; told me also that he was just tryin' to live up to how you and his momma dun raised him. That oughta make ya proud to hear what I just told ya, huh?"

"Yes, Louis, it does do just that!" Jacob continued to smile at his son with a great deal of pride.

William still did not believe what Louis had just told him about why he had come to Maine. "Come on, Johnny Reb, why ya here? Did ya come up here by steamer or by railroad? Stop funning me, what's the real reason you're here? And tell me another thing too, what happened after I left ya at the hospital? Where else did ya do some fighting in the war after ya healed up?"

"I didn't do no more fightin', William, wasn't up to it for a long time neither. I spent a few months just recovering in Gettysburg after y'all left. Got treated there by some Catholic nuns who belonged to some religious order; might have been the Sisters of Charity if I recall properly. Right fine folks they were. Nursed me back to somewhat decent health at the Lutheran Seminary right there in Gettysburg; that's where a lot of our boys were cared for. Started to feel good about my injuries, and then I had a relapse with my hip here. Took time to recover after they dun sewed me back together as my hip injury got infected real bad. Also took some time for my broken ribs to heal as well. Some doc thought they likely got busted up when them two other soldiers had fallen on me." Pausing for a moment, Louis then looked at William and asked him a question that brought them both back to Little Round Top. "Do ya recall pulling them dead boys off of me that day?" The simple nod of the head he saw told Louis the day had been remembered by his friend. "When I was finally able to walk, I was still pretty weak so they were kind enough to let me stay for another two weeks to get my strength back. About that time, and I have to tell ya this cause it's the truth, but I kinda lost interest in the war. Seen too many men, good men they was, get either killed or hurt badly from the fightin' that was being dun. Well, after I kinda snuck out of Gettysburg, as I weren't too keen on spending the rest of the war in one of your prison camps, I just started walkin' south, knew I'd run into our boys sooner or later. Finally got to see a couple of our army doctors, and after they looked over my hip injury, they told me to go home and rest until I was better. Mind ya, I didn't try to sway their opinion none about that! Went back home, rested some until I was better, and then the war was almost over. About the time I was fixin' to leave to come see ya, my cousin, Eddie, showed back home. Ya never met him, but he was with me at Little Round Top. He got taken prisoner at the end of the day when you fellas charged at us with them dang bayonets of yours. He spent the rest of the war in some prison camp y'all had someplace. He lost a bunch of weight there, but he'll be fine after eatin' some of his momma's country cookin'. I'm fixin' to spend some time with him when I get back home, but for right now I'm here with y'all!"

Still not hearing all of the answers to his questions, William pressed Louis for more information. "Come on, Louis, are ya gonna tell us how ya managed to get all the way up here from Alabama? Was it by steamer or railroad, or how?"

For a few brief moments, Louis sheepishly smiled before finally answering the question. "I walked mostly. Hitched a few rides here and there, but mostly I walked. Don't like boats, and I ain't too trustin' of trains, so mostly I walked. It was a long journey north!"

Not believing what he heard, William questioned Louis on what he had just said. "You didn't walk all the way here from Alabama just to see me! How'd ya really get here?"

Louis smiled at the incredulous look he saw on his friend's face. "Like I just dun told ya, William, I walked. Well, seems like I dun walked the whole way anyhow. Rode my horse till it got stolen from me outside of Columbia. That's there in South Carolina, if y'all don't know. Stolen, I do believe, by some Georgia boys I dun met earlier that day. They was makin' their way home from the war; got tired of walkin' I figured. They dun stole it from me whiles I was sleepin'! Reckon I ain't got no more use for Georgia boys, even if they did fight alongside of me in the war a couple of times. Ain't right to steal a man's horse! No, sir, it ain't!" Pausing for a moment as he reflected back on his horse being stolen, Louis then finished telling William and his father about the rest of his trip.

"Took me the better part of three months, but I did it. Walked mostly from that point on, but I gots me a few rides in some hay wagons and such. Got lucky a couple of times when I caught some rides across a few rivers by some downright nice fellas who pulled rafts across the water for a livin'. Had to wade and swim over a few more, but it weren't bad. Spent some days and nights just walkin', and I spent some days taking it easy, just being lazy so I could give my feet some rest. Even spent three days helpin' a farmer in Maple Hill, North Carolina work his farm. Coming through North Carolina I met Mr. Thomas Larson, a right neighborly type of person, who offered me a meal as I was passing by his place."

Pausing for a moment as he thought of meeting Thomas, a big smile crossed over Louis' face. "Mr. Larson, he's a big strong man, one of the biggest I ever dun seen. He told me about losing his only son during the war. Son's name was Michael; got himself killed during the Battle of Winchester. That's Winchester, Virginia, if y'all don't know. The boy died there last September, fighting under General Jubal Early. Felt bad for the man so I stayed a few days and helped him get his corn crop planted for the season. Made me feel good about what I dun for him, just like it musta made you feel when ya got me to the hospital that day. Feels good when ya help folks in times of need, don't it?" Louis and William exchanged smiles with each other as they recalled the specific good deeds they each had been a part of. "Met some nice folks on the long walk up here, good Yankee folks too, just like y'all! Giving some thought to stopping and seeing Mr. Larson, and perhaps a few of them other folks I met, when I head for home. Thought it be nice to see them again, perhaps sit a spell with each of them and just rest for a time. Ain't got no real plans though, guess I'll go where my feet takes me!"

William had enjoyed listening to his friend talk, but he still had trouble believing that Louis had come this entire way just to see him. "Louis, ya really came that entire way just to see me? I mean ya thanked me for helping ya when I left the hospital that day."

"I come up to see ya for the reasons we been talking about. I come to see ya to thank ya proper for what ya dun for me. Saving a man's life is a special thing, so I figured I had to say thanks to ya the right way. I'm a Southerner, and right proud of it, and whiles I don't proclaim to know too much about y'all up here in this part of the country, us southern folks don't forget when someone helps them through a tough time. That's what ya dun for me, helped me through a real tough time. No tellin' what would have happened to me if ya didn't come along like ya did that morning. Might have died right there, I suppose. I likely could have sent ya a letter or a telegraph message, but that didn't seem like the right thing to be doing. A man has to say thank you to a friend in person, just like I'm doing right now. Can't think of another proper way to show my appreciation than by doing it the way I'm doing. Wanted to thank ya personal like, and now I have. Guess I can start for home now."

Hearing Louis talk about coming to Maine to thank him for helping him during the war was difficult enough for William to comprehend, but hearing his friend talk about leaving for home so soon was something that wasn't going to happen. "What? Ya just got here! Ya ain't leaving without meeting my ma, and tasting some of her fine cooking. You and me are gonna do a few things together for a couple of days before ya even start to think about heading for home, right pa?"

William's father quickly piped in and supported his son's comments. "He's right, Louis. What ya done coming all this way, well . . . let's just say that's something special ya done for William. Listen to me when I tell ya that northern folks ain't much different than you southern folks as we got our own ways of doing things proper also. I ain't having my son's friend leave without him staying with us for a few days. Stay as long as ya like as we'd be pleased to have ya. William's right about his ma's cooking; she's a right fine cook! Ya like lobsters? She makes them a half-a-dozen different ways. I'm gonna have one or two on the table for ya tonight!"

It took William and Jacob a couple of minutes to convince Louis to stay on for a few days, but finally he agreed to be their guest. As Jacob busied himself so they could lock the boathouse up and then be on their way home, William asked his friend a question he had just thought of. "Louis, did ya ever give a thought that I might not have been here when ya got here? I could have been killed in the war, or I could have been off someplace else when ya got here. What would ya have done then?"

Louis thought for a moment before answering William's question. Sheepishly he finally answered it. "That's a good question, Billy Yank! Can't say I gave it a moment's thought about ya not being here. Guess I likely would have sat here talkin' with your pappy until ya dun got here!"

The response made William laugh, and soon his friend joined in. Louis really had never given a moment's thought to his friend not being in Maine when he got there.

As he helped his father finish closing up the boathouse, William hollered to his friend from across the wide building. "Come on, Louis, grab that raggedy looking set of saddlebags of yours, and let's go see my ma. I'm hungry, bet you are too!"

"Hold on, Billy Yank! Bring your pa over here. I's got something to give ya."

As William and his father walked back to where Louis had been standing, they saw him kneel down on the floor and begin to rummage through his saddlebags. Quickly finished searching in his bag for what he had been looking for, he stood up as Jacob and his son got back to where he was waiting for them. As they did, they both could see that Louis was holding a revolver in his right hand.

"I want ya to have this, William, I want it to come back home." Louis then handed the gun, a Colt .31 caliber revolver, to his friend.

After looking over the revolver for a few moments, and after asking Louis where he had gotten it, William handed the empty gun to his father to inspect.

"Them Georgia boys who stole my horse had it with them. Them boys claimed they got it from one of your Union officers when they captured him someplace during the war. Not sure if what them horse thieves told me is true or not, but it sure looks to be a Yankee's gun. Look at the bottom of them grips, it's got them initials right there. See there, it's got 'F.G.W. – CT' carved nicely in the wood. Likely dun belonged to a Connecticut boy, I guess. Traded them dang fools some grub I had for the gun. Thought ya might like to have it. At least I got it back to a fella Yankee!"

Louis' last comment caused William to smile back at his friend. He appreciated the gesture his friend had made in giving him the small gun. "Thanks, Louis, maybe someday I'll even try and find out who owned it. Be hard to do, but I might give it a try. If I can find him, I'll be glad to let him know a Reb got it back for him!"

Just as his friend had done for him, William surprised Louis with a similar gift. Walking over to a small wooden cabinet, he returned carrying the saber he had found on one of the slopes at Little Round Top. He had found it the day that he had discovered Louis lying injured on the side of the hill.

"Louis, I found this here saber the day we first met. There's a good chance that it belonged to one of your officers as I found it lying next to one. Kinda funny, this here saber also has something scratched into the knuckle bow area. I ain't never been able to make out the letters, but when you look at it later you'll see what I'm talkin' about. Like you said about the revolver, I feel the same way about this. I want it to go home to Alabama with ya. Keep it as a souvenir or something."

Looking at the saber soon brought a few tears to Louis' eyes as the day of fighting at Little Round Top had caused him to lose many of his friends. "Much obliged, William, much obliged. I'll be pleased to bring it back home."

******

Louis stayed with William and his family for another five days before heading home to Alabama. Despite their efforts, the Barton family could not convince him to let them pay his way home by steamer or train, or to let them buy him a horse for the ride home. It had been difficult enough just to get him to accept the burlap bag of food William's mother had made for him.

"Nope, no thank ya, but I do appreciate the offer! My feets got me here, and they's gettin' me home as well. I sure do appreciate the hospitality y'all dun shown me. It's a memory that I'll keep for the rest of my days."

After a hearty breakfast, and after inviting William and his parents to come visit him, Louis gave the Barton family a wave goodbye and headed back to his beloved Alabama. Like the memories he carried home from Maine, he would bring a few more home with him from his long walk through several states.

******

Three more times in their lives, William and Louis would meet again. Once would be at the fiftieth reunion of the Battle of Gettysburg, and once would be when William travelled to Alabama to visit his friend in the summer of 1893. Through the years they would communicate with each other by letters, packages, and even occasionally by telegraph. Both would marry, and each would have three boys of their own. They would each name their oldest son after the friend they had made at Gettysburg. Living until 1916, they would die in their respective home states a scant six months apart from each other.

They had met during the brutality of the American Civil War, but their friendship had survived for years after the war had ended.

They each had survived the long journey north.

AFTERWORD

"I am now a Yankee General, formerly a Rebel Colonel, and right each time!"

BRIGADIER GENERAL WILLIAM C. OATES AFTER RECEIVING
HIS 1898 SPANISH-AMERICAN WAR COMMISSION
FROM PRESIDENT WILLIAM MCKINLEY.

In the years that followed the war, many of the soldiers who fought at Gettysburg would meet at the many various reunions that were held. Doing so allowed many of the war's combatants to become friends, and to allow the soldiers of the two opposing sides to gain at least a partial respect for why they each had fought for their causes like they had.

While many of the soldiers tamed their hate and contempt for each other just like William and Louis had done, two other men struggled somewhat against each other in the years after the war.

After Gettysburg, General Joshua Lawrence Chamberlain, and the 20th Maine, would fight in many more battles. They would fight during the Mine Run Campaign, during the Battle of the Wilderness, at the Siege of Petersburg, and in many other places. It was partially due to his accomplishments throughout the war that had caused Chamberlain to be selected by General Grant to receive the formal surrender of the Confederate troops at Appomattox Court House.

During the war, Chamberlain would take part in twenty-four battles, and have a role in many other reconnaissance missions and skirmishes. His men would help capture approximately 2,700 Confederate prisoners and eight battle flags.

As the brigade commander for the Union's Fifth Corps – First Brigade, on June 18, 1864, at Rives Salient, Chamberlain received his most serious wound. It would occur during a day of fighting when his 20th Maine had been held in reserve. Despite being seriously wounded, he stayed in the battle until he finally collapsed from the loss of blood.

He later would be taken aboard the *U.S.S. Connecticut* and taken to Annapolis for additional care. Two days after receiving his most serious wound, and one at first that was thought to be a mortal wound, Grant promoted Chamberlain to Brigadier General.

After the war, despite struggling at times with health issues from the six times he was wounded in fighting, Chamberlain would live a long and prosperous life in Maine. He would live there for many years, and would accomplish many more tasks, before finally passing from this life in 1914.

For his efforts at Little Round Top, Chamberlain would be awarded the Medal of Honor for *"conspicuous personal gallantry and distinguished service"*. He would serve four consecutive one-year terms as a Republican governor of Maine, and would enjoy great popularity during his time in office from 1867 to 1870. Later, he would serve as president of Bowdoin College for twelve years, and would teach an additional two years after concluding his time as the school's president.

Following his time at Bowdoin, and after spending time as a writer, Chamberlain received an appointment, in 1900, from President William McKinley to be the Surveyor of the Port of Portland.

******

Like his adversary at Little Round Top, Colonel William C. Oates would also do well in life after Gettysburg. Like Chamberlain, Oates was also wounded six times during the war. His most serious injury occurred on August 16, 1864, in fighting at Fussell's Mills, Virginia. In that battle a Yankee minie ball severely wounded him. The wound would later cause him to lose his right arm. This would be his final injury of the war; one that would knock him out of the war due to health issues.

Back in Alabama after the war, Oates, the wiregrass raised son of Pike County, would become a very popular figure as both a lawyer and as a politician. In the 1870's, he was elected to the Alabama House of Representatives. In 1880, he was elected to the United States House of Representatives where he would serve seven consecutive terms.

As Chamberlain had been elected governor of Maine, Oates would also be elected governor of Alabama, serving one two-year term after his days in Washington had come to an end.

Like he did for Chamberlain, President McKinley also gave Oates a job late in life as well. In 1898, McKinley commissioned him as a Brigadier General during the Spanish – American War. He would later command three different brigades that were stateside during the war, but would never see any wartime action. His days fighting in military wars had long been over.

******

In the years after the war, Chamberlain took several opportunities to promote, and possibly enhance, both the reputation and the role that the Union's Fifth Corps played during the fighting that had occurred at Little Round Top. Most notably, it was often done when speaking or writing about the roles that he and the 20th Maine had played there.

As Oates and Chamberlain had pride in the roles their regiments played at Gettysburg, their opinions, and their differences, would carry on during the years that followed the war. They would be differences that never would be settled.

When others, including Oates, tried to imply that the bayonet charge Chamberlain had ordered at Little Round Top played a smaller role in the outcome of the battle that day, Chamberlain refused to listen to the points they had raised. For those who also pointed out that the 15th Alabama was exhausted from days of marching prior to reaching Gettysburg, that they were also exhausted from the repeated attacks they had made up the steep slopes of Little Round Top, and that the Alabamians had fought for an extended period of time with little or no drinking water, Chamberlain also refused to listen to any of those points that were raised as well. To his dying day, he believed the 20th Maine, as well as his own actions in ordering the bayonet charge, had saved the day for the Union army.

The simple fact is, that while Chamberlain and the 20th Maine were heroes that day, many others were as well. Chamberlain and the 20th Maine each simply played a role in the defense of Little Round Top, just like those many other Union soldiers who also helped to beat back the repeated attacks made by the 15th Alabama, and others. The day's success not only belonged to the soldiers from Maine, but also belonged to those soldiers from Pennsylvania, New York, and Michigan, and to other individuals like Vincent, Warren, Meade, and several others. In many events in life these days, successes are often called 'Team Efforts'; in the case of Little Round Top it was truly a 'Brigade Effort'.

As the country learned more and more about the fighting that had occurred at Gettysburg, efforts began to memorialize the events of this three-day battle. Among those efforts was one to honor the 15th Alabama at Little Round Top. While Chamberlain never refuted the courage and bravery that the 15th Alabama had displayed that day, and while he often spoke and wrote about how well those soldiers had fought, he did refute a claim that Oates had presented to others.

After Oates had identified to others where the 15th Alabama had gotten to during their assaults on the 20th Maine's position, Chamberlain, after learning of the alleged high water mark for the Confederacy that day, rebuked Oates' claim. He simply refused to accept the position Oates had claimed the 15th Alabama had reached that day. Despite many efforts to mediate a solution to the dispute, it was never resolved. While the monuments and the history of Gettysburg reflect the heroism displayed by the 20th Maine on Day Two of the battle, the monument to recognize the brave efforts of the 15th Alabama was never erected. While Chamberlain did not oppose a monument being placed where the Alabamians had fought that day, he would never allow it to be placed close to where his men had stood tall that day.

In his later years, like he had done in his written report that detailed the fighting his men had done at Little Round Top, Oates often fondly recalled the fighting prowess of the 15th Alabama. One of his most famous quotes reflects the pride he had in that group of men. "There was no better regiment in the Confederate Army than the Fifteenth Alabama, and when properly commanded, if it failed to carry any point against which it was thrown, no other single regiment need try it."

One of the men that typified the fighting spirit of Oates' 15th Alabama was Sgt. Patrick O'Connor. Born in Ireland, like many soldiers who fought in the war, he would fight bravely for the Confederacy.

After fighting at Gettysburg, he would fight in several more battles, and would be promoted on two more occasions, the last being to Second Lieutenant. It was a promotion he received just days prior to Christmas, 1863. Lt. O'Connor, from Eufaula, Alabama, who had joined the 15th Alabama at the age of 23, would later be killed in action at Cold Harbor, Virginia, in June, 1864. Like so many other men from his generation, he would die far too young.

******

Despite his influence as the Commissioner for Locating and Marking Confederate Graves in the North, an appointment he received from President Theodore Roosevelt, and despite working with many various commissioners of the Gettysburg National Military Park, Oates was never able to convince the powers to be to honor his 15th Alabama with a monument on Little Round Top. Unlike so many others who had fought so bravely at Little Round Top, the 15th Alabama has never been so honored with a monument of their own. Oates' inability to have a monument erected there for his men, and for his fallen brother, was one of his most frustrating moments in life.

On September 9, 1910, Colonel William C. Oates passed from this life to the next. In his passing, just as Maine would do for Chamberlain when he died in February, 1914, the people of Alabama remembered their native son for all he had done for their state, for the South, and for the people of the United States.

Unlike William and Louis, the two Civil War soldiers who faded from view after they each had passed away, Chamberlain and Oates would remain as figures in American History for the generations that followed theirs.

CPSIA information can be obtained at www.ICGtesting.com
Printed in the USA
LVOW131024140413

328976LV00005B/5/P